A Magical
Girl Retires

A Magical Girl Retires

PARK SEOLYEON

TRANSLATED BY ANTON HUR

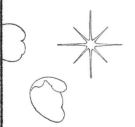

HarperVia

An Imprint of HarperCollins*Publishers*

This book is published with the support of the Literature Translation Institute of Literature (LTI Korea).

HarperCollins books may be purchased for educational, business, or sales promotional use. For information, please email the Special Markets Department at SPsales@harpercollins.com.

Originally published as *Mabopssonyo euntwehamnida* in South Korea in 2022 by Changbi Publishers.

FIRST HARPERVIA EDITION PUBLISHED APRIL 2024

Designed by Yvonne Chan
Illustrations on p. iii © Pixxsa/stock.adobe.com
Unless otherwise noted, illustrations provided by Kim Sanho

Library of Congress Cataloging-in-Publication Data has been applied for.

ISBN 978-0-06-337326-6
ISBN 978-0-06-341637-6 (ANZ)

24 25 26 27 28 LBC 10 9 8 7 6

Contents

A Magical Girl Retires

Destined to Be a Magical Girl

What's the best way to die that would create the least amount of annoyance for everyone else?

I think I've worked hard enough at life—I wasn't given much, but I tried my best not to waste any of it, at least. But even as I've come this far on my own two feet, I can't help but feel other people have been pushing me along all the way.

The wait number dispensed to me at the bank was 777.

Twenty-nine.

Doesn't everyone feel like this at that age?

I once read an article online titled "Thirty-Six Questions That Lead to Love." It was in the *New York Times*, and evidently, any couple who answered these thirty-six questions together was bound to end up in love. Question #7 went like this:

"Do you have a secret hunch about how you will die?"

I'm probably going to die without anyone knowing. That's my hope and also what's probably going to happen. It's the one wish in my life that I honestly feel has any chance of coming true.

And the opportunity for this wish to come true is very close at hand.

TUESDAY, 3:00 A.M., MAPO BRIDGE IN WESTERN SEOUL

An average of 0.3 cars per minute zoomed by, taking for granted their right to move at the speed of bullets at this hour. As I sit leaning against the railings, I'm certain none of their drivers have seen me. I have been sitting here for the past two hours. The last time a pedestrian passed by was about forty minutes before. I could tell they were drunk even from afar (Who else would cross this long bridge in the middle of the night—someone in their right mind?), but afraid of being bothered, I hugged my legs so tight my heels touched my behind. I stopped breathing.

Given this stumbling, drunk person had passed right in front of me, I figured he'd had plenty of time to notice my presence, but he seemed not to. He was walking slower than I had expected, and so I had to gasp for breath as soon as he passed me—*pah!*—but he didn't look back. Which, weirdly, made me sad. Was I *invisible*? Had someone pressed the mute button on me?

Maybe my gasp sounded louder to me than it actually was. I was wearing a mask, after all; it could have muffled the sound. I'd been imagining he would discover me and pick a fight and—*oh no oh no oh nooooooo*—one of us would push the other over the railings, but once he simply passed by without incident, I felt not relief but sadness . . . How odd. Not that I couldn't exactly understand why. After all, I hadn't only imagined the man and me struggling against the railing—I had another fantasy that alcohol had unfurled the man's busybody flag, and he would ask me why I was sitting here alone crying and be concerned for me.

I'm such an idiot.

The tears that had paused began to flow again; I drank

some water, and feeling pathetic about how I'd come here to throw myself in the river yet was drinking water because I felt thirsty, I threw the plastic bottle over the railing . . . That was half an hour ago. Sorry for polluting the environment. I'm the real pollution. But then I started feeling thirsty again and regretted my decision. Why did I throw away my water? Maybe I was just born to regret everything.

It was exactly three years ago that I tried to think of a way to kill myself without being a nuisance. Which means I was not the unhappiest person in the world. If I were truly unhappy, I would've thought up ways to die much earlier than that. Grandfather always used to say, *The world is full of people who are worse off than ourselves—so when someone asks for help, you have to help them as much as you can. That's building virtue. Virtue that will help me when I'm in the afterlife and your mother and even your father . . .*

But Grandfather, I've really thought about it, and I think if someone like me sets out to help anyone, I'll only do more harm than good.

There's something I've been carrying around in my pocket for a while. Nothing special, just a slip of paper with the number 777 printed on it, my waiting-in-line number at the bank. Like it's a talisman of good luck. That day I took that number out of the machine, I thought I was having a lucky day. It was the first time I had ever applied for a credit card. Isn't it amazing that I could even own a credit card? You weren't there, Grandfather, to pay off my loans anymore, but now I could buy things in zero-fee installments of three months, sometimes even up to seven months. My hands were shaking a little and I felt almost scared; that's how happy I was. There was a little bin at the teller window where you were supposed to throw away your crumpled ticket, but I pretended I didn't see it and snuck my number out of the bank.

I don't think I had many worries when I had a job. I'd been using my debit card, which took money right out of my account at every use, but I had simply changed this method to getting a bill at the end of the month and pay-ing later. Every payday was me being paid for work done the month before anyway. I loved the fact that I didn't have to save up to buy; I could buy first and pay it off little by little. There wasn't a fridge in my apartment, you see. Since I didn't have a fridge, I couldn't cook anything, and that meant wasting money eating out. These days I don't even remember how I lived without a fridge, but I'll never forget how happy I felt when it was delivered. Now that I had this fridge, everything would get better little by little, I thought. I still don't hold the slightest bit of resentment toward the fridge.

I don't really think I spent that much money. All I did was live my life and the debt just accumulated. Well, the pandemic costing me my job was the biggest thing. Thankfully, I had enough money to pay off my bills for that last month, but there were still three installments left on the fridge.

I've been thinking about this lately—even if the pandemic didn't happen, and I never lost my job, I probably would've gone bankrupt anyway. It's just that instead of becoming poorer in increments too small to be noticed, I happened to really crash into it, saving me some time.

I had an interview yesterday. I really wanted to get the job; it was for a full-time position this time around, which made me a little excited about it. But I couldn't find the 777 I'd been carrying around with me like a talisman. It wasn't in the pockets of the clothes I'd worn the day before or stuck under the magnet on the fridge—looking for it made me almost late for the interview. Because

I'm not stupid enough to think looking for one's lucky number is more important than getting to an interview on time, I just gave up and left. And because there's no washing machine in my apartment, I wore the fancy, neat clothing I had washed and dried in the coin laundromat. If I'd saved up the money I'd spent on the laundromat, I would've been able to afford a small used washing machine, but my apartment is so small there isn't really a place to put one . . .

What have you been doing all this time at your age? That's what the interviewer said to me. I sat on a stool being interviewed by some midlevel manager at that company, and he spoke so loudly that I'm sure everyone heard what he said. *How can your résumé be this short when you're a whole twenty-nine years old?* He probably felt no compunction saying that out loud. Because he wasn't wrong. As I left the building later, holding back my tears, I put my hands in my pockets and felt a piece of paper there. A wad of pulp, torn and mushed, with the number 7 just barely visible on one side.

My unpaid credit card debt is a little over three million won.

You probably don't know this, Grandfather, but credit

cards have this thing called a "revolving balance"—like, *Oh, you don't have the means to pay your bill? Then all you have to do is pay back what you can afford right now! Hmm, what about 20 percent? You can do that, right? Too much? All right, then 10 percent? I don't think we can go lower than that. Okay, the rest we can stick a little more interest on and send it off to the next month. But you better do better next month!* That kind of thing. How incredibly polite they sound, right? But weirdly enough, the revolving balance is set to increase little by little. The short-term work I managed to get can barely make the minimum payments on it.

Maybe it's the name that makes me think I'm playing Russian roulette with someone I can't see. Grandfather, do you know what Russian roulette is? It's a game where people take turns pulling the trigger on a revolver that has one bullet. *Whew, I made it through this month. The gun didn't go off. But will it next month?* That's kind of what it feels like. It's money I actually spent, so I can't blame anyone else but myself for this mess, but the whole thing just makes my head feel like it's going to explode any minute.

Staying alive costs money . . . It took me way too long to realize this simple truth.

I guess everyone would think I was a loser for thinking about killing myself over three million won. But I think this is just the beginning. My credit card limit is still the same as it was when I first made it: five million won. So, what's the point of living another month or two? Waiting for my debt to go up to five million, for the bullet to finally fire? Even I think it's pathetic, choosing suicide because of three million won. And that's why I wanted no one to know I was dead. Because I want no one to know why I died. Even if they did know, I hope they pretend they didn't. Because it's just too embarrassing.

On the way to the bridge, I'd bought a notepad at a convenience store and cried big fat tears as I tried to leave something behind. I could barely write down all the thoughts that were pouring through my mind. In my effort to embarrass myself in writing as little as possible, I ended up writing, *I'm sorry, Grandfather*, and there was nothing left to write, and it occurred to me that writing anything down went against my trying to kill myself without anyone knowing, that the only way for me to get my wish was if no one knew it was me who died . . .

Other than that, dawn was going to break soon, and the

trains would begin to run, so I told myself I had to do the deed as quickly as possible.

At least there are no cars, I thought—then a taxi happened to zoom by. Jesus, nothing was going my way! Oh, who cares . . . It's the end anyway . . .

I bent down and put my notepad on the ground, turned around slowly, and then saw the taxi that had just passed me was still on the bridge. And it was . . . getting closer. It had taken a U-turn and was coming back on the wrong side of the road. *Wait, are they allowed to do that? I know there are no cars coming, but . . . Are they coming to run me over?* Despite this thought, I couldn't move.

As I hesitated, the taxi stopped right in front of me. The woman who got out of the backseat was wearing a cute white dress that came down to her knees, and she had on white shoes and a white bow. What the hell . . . angel cosplay? The streetlamps, which I hadn't noticed at all until that moment, seemed to be spotlighting her—she glowed white.

"It is not your destiny to die now."

Chills. *How did she know I was trying to kill myself?*

The realization came later that anyone passing by could've guessed that was what I was trying to do. But when I say "later," I mean the point where I understood that this woman, who was named Ah Roa, had known exactly where I would be and came to find me at just the right time.

But back then, when I didn't know anything, the only thought that came to mind was that this was a *miracle*, and I burst into tears.

"You . . . you know about my destiny?" I asked.

"Of course."

Her voice was so trustworthy, so pleasant. Ah Roa came up to me and took my hand, her touch as gentle as someone handling something fragile.

"Your destiny is to become a magical girl."

The Greatest Magical Girl in the World

Me? A magical girl?"

I'd seen them on television. Not the ones in cartoons waving their magic wands and transforming into powerful beings—or into powerful outfits—and vanquishing monsters and aliens, but the ones on the news. Those who use their superpowers or magic or whatever to rout out criminals and rescue people in dire need. The difference between the magical girls in animation and on the news is whether their enemies are imaginary nuisances or real-life evil and disasters. Like capturing bank robbers using their summoning spells and stopping car accidents with their telekinesis.

From what I understand, there were two reasons why we called them "magical girls" instead of using that other pop culture cliché, "superhero." One, they themselves asked to be called magical girls. Two, this magic only seemed to manifest in girls. Therefore . . .

"I . . . don't think I'm young enough to be a magical girl?"

The taxi was rapidly but smoothly zipping off the bridge, and the angelic beauty who had seated me next to her in the backseat was rummaging through her handbag. The handbag was completely white, like the woman's clothes, and it had a coin-purse-like clasp that snapped shut with a satisfying *tak*.

The woman turned to me and asked, "How old do I look?"

"How old are you?"

"That's a secret."

I could almost see the outlines of her smile behind her white mask. I'd thought she was a little strange, but . . . this was really silly.

She held out a card. "This is who I am."

TRADE UNION FOR MAGICAL GIRLS

OFFICER AH ROA

Obviously, she didn't write her age on the card.

"It's true most of the magical girls out there are girls," she said. "But not all magical girls are girls. You don't have to look like a girl on the outside to become aware of your gift, and it's not like we don't age after we come into our calling."

I think I had heard that the longest-working magical girl was old enough to be called Grandmother.

"When is the proper age to shed the moniker 'girl'? Do you stop being one with your first period? Are you an adult once you grow taller than 160 centimeters? When lots of adults don't reach that height anyway? And is it not true that all of our girlhoods are different, not just in terms of physical growth, but in the growth of our hearts and minds?"

She had a point. I mean, when did my own girlhood begin and end, exactly? I couldn't quite circle a lasso around it, but I knew, at least, when it had ended. Three years ago, when Grandfather died. To be fair, I was already beyond the age one can call oneself a girl, but at least until that moment I hadn't thought of myself as particularly grown-up. Because it was all right not to. Up until then.

"They say great power comes with great responsibility. There are many complicated things happening to magical girls. Things like liability for property damage during their activities or being denied insurance coverage. Magical girls of legal age have it even worse. The other cases I just mentioned might be mitigated by having a legal guardian, but an adult magical girl has to take care of everything on her own. Which is why we needed a union."

Her mention of insurance, as well as her silver-tongued delivery of her spiel, made me instantly wonder if she was trying to sell me health insurance.

"And what does this have to do with me again?" I asked.

"With our new focus on collective action, we've also begun to invest in the discovery and education of new magical girls."

Roa showed me the other object she held in her hand. It looked like a cosmetic compact, its rim shimmering in rainbow colors. In the little mirror, my face reflected back at me.

"Uh . . . What about this thing?"

"Doesn't it seem a little different to you?"

Roa held the mirror this way and that. Come to think of it, my reflection wasn't exactly mine. My eyes weren't red and puffy from crying, and I also was not wearing a mask. I looked so much like my normal self that it seemed almost ridiculous I hadn't noticed right away. It looked like a very good passport photo, right there inside Roa's compact.

"This is my talisman," Roa said. "I call it the Ahroamirror."

"Why . . . is my face inside it?"

"It proves you're destined to be a magical girl."

Just as she had on the bridge, she gripped my hand.

"That's my talent."

What was her talent? Holding strangers' hands? Showing people images of themselves in the mirror? Unable to look at Roa and the Ahroamirror at the same time, my eyes kept going back and forth between them, until Roa cleared her throat.

"Let me introduce myself. I am Ah Roa, the Clairvoyant Magical Girl. An officer of the union whose mission is to find the greatest magical girl in the world."

At that moment, I couldn't check my expression through the Ahroamirror—why on earth had I thought it was a mirror in the first place, how odd—but I'm sure my face might as well have had the words *So what* writ large across it. But when I heard what Roa had to say next, it all made sense. It was like my whole life, not just this car ride, had been building up until this moment.

"We believe that the Magical Girl of Time is the greatest magical girl of all."

They say it's a calling when it seems like you're born to do something because you happen to be so good at it. When I was a girl, I wanted to be a watchmaker. Well, I still want to be one—I don't think it's too late.

When I looked up the profession on the internet, it told me watchmakers needed to become watch designers first. That it wasn't enough to know how to put watch parts together, that I would need to come up with a watch design that had never been seen before. How incredible is that? I couldn't wait to get started.

Grandfather had owned a jewelry store, which meant this was a way for me to take on the family job, in a way. Having looked over his shoulder since I was a middle school student, I knew how to change watch straps and knobs. By the time I got to high school, I got pretty good at more complicated fixes, and even the most sharp-eyed customer couldn't catch on to the fact that it was me and not Grandfather who had fixed their watches, leading Grandfather and me to do many a high five behind our customers' backs. *Grandfather, I just love watches. When I look at them, I just . . . It's like they're a whole universe. The universe itself. Even the smallest watch.*

When Grandfather sat there in his store, he looked like he was rich with time, the walls and displays covered with watches and clocks and such. My favorite clock in the store hung across from the cash register. It was a world clock made up of five faces. They moved at different but synchronized angles, reminding us that time did not rest anywhere on Earth.

Grandfather told me about the best jewelry school in East Asia, which happened to be in Japan. Throughout my teen years, it was my goal to get into that school. Grandfather even said he would help me any way he could. That I would have to work really hard to show him I was serious about becoming a watch designer. *Of course!* I thought. I studied Japanese, saved up for my future tuition and board, and helped Grandfather at the store whenever I could. My homeroom teacher wrote in my transcript: *No real interest in her studies but a very diligent, polite, and goal-oriented student.* Even then, Grandfather called me a genius. That was enough. The person I loved and respected the most in the world called me a genius; therefore, I was a genius.

Which was why Roa's words made me feel like she was talking directly to me. That I'd thought I was born to make watches but turned out to be the destined Magical Girl of Time would sound about right to anyone. Especially to me, who took in this news with the satisfaction of hearing that *click* when a watch you've assembled starts to tick off the seconds. And to think it was all about me . . .

I was so excited I almost forgot I was trying to die not too long ago.

"The Magical Girl of Time?"

I asked her this one more time because I wanted, for once, to hear someone else say that I was an important person, that I mattered. Roa did not disappoint.

"Yes, the person who can control time is also the person who can truly become the greatest magical girl."

Her grip, which had never let go of me, grew stronger.

"I'm the Clairvoyant Magical Girl who can find those who have not come into their power, and it was my mirror that showed me who you were. Your image appeared more clearly in my Ahroamirror than anything I have ever seen. Do you understand what I mean?"

They say the number of humans who have ever lived on this planet is over a hundred billion. Since it was about ten years ago when I heard this, I'm sure that number has only gone up. And the number of people who have died must also have gone past a hundred billion. Which means if I had died as I'd intended, I would've been . . . the hundred billion and somethingth person to leave this world. I know this isn't a fact to smile about, but it feels like I've won a marathon countless billions—or hundred billions—were running in. I must've been far ahead of my parents, even Grandfather, and so many millions and billions of people were between us we would never be able to find each other in the crowd.

Which means if they weren't going to be first anyway, they hadn't needed to be in such a hurry . . .

After I got out of the taxi and closed my apartment door behind me, I leaned my back against it and slid down to the floor.

Grandfather, they say I'm a magical girl.

The Magical Girl of Time, the greatest ever.

That's . . . me?

I shook my head and stuck Roa's card on the fridge with a magnet where my lucky 777 bank ticket had been, where Roa's name sparkled in the slice of dawning light that entered through the window of the basement apartment.

As if it were a signal that the magic had already begun.

A Sustainable Magical Girl

Four days passed before I called Roa. If you were to ask me what I did during those four days . . . I did nothing. I searched the news for magical girl stuff and looked in the fridge when I became unbearably hungry, so it's not like I did *nothing* nothing, but I really didn't do much else to prepare for my life ahead.

The reason it took me four days to call was that I just couldn't summon the courage. Roa had told me what a great person I was to become, but this was before anything to that effect had happened, and there was something embarrassing about calling her when nothing had happened . . . But to be honest, I needed Roa for the same reason. Becoming a magical girl was surely not as simple as declaring oneself as one, not that I wasn't grateful for her saving my life on the bridge and all, but I did require some follow-up and guidance.

The Clairvoyant Magical Girl Ah Roa—she must've known on some level I would be this way, as well as the reason why I would spend four days worrying about whether I should call or not.

If we were to talk about courage, I'm like . . . a used-up tube of toothpaste. Unless I squeeze out the tiny bits that are left in my body and mind, nothing will leave my mouth—and the tiny bit that does manage to leave the tube shoots into the air and becomes wasted anyway.

"I was waiting for you to call," Roa said instead of saying hello.

I was grateful to her and surprised. Maybe this was why the response I spent four days rehearsing went out the window, and I blurted out something else.

"What's so great about becoming a magical girl?"

Once I said it, I suddenly realized what I had been so worried about. Becoming a magical girl was one thing, but if I was left with my revolving balance of three million won (and rising), all the magical girling in the world wouldn't make a difference.

"I'm on my way to get you."

"Excuse me?" *That didn't answer my question!*

"Like I said, I was waiting for you. I'll show you what you need to see. I'm sure you'll love it."

Just as I thought on the night Roa took me home, it seemed weird to think about someone as fancy as her coming to my decrepit banjiha basement apartment and knocking on the door. I quickly showered and put on my clothes, but Roa showed up in just half an hour. It was embarrassing; let's just say the way my apartment smelled wasn't very magical or girly.

After four days of staying inside, being outside felt strange. The sun was up, but weirdly hazy; while it wasn't too strong, it was humid and hot. It was already late spring, sure, but why was it so hot? A little self-conscious about my damp armpits, I followed Roa into a taxi.

"Let me tell you what's so great about becoming a magical girl."

I had an idea about her methods at this point. Because here she was, holding my hand in hers, speaking to me in her pleasant voice. And there I was, understanding only about half of what was going on, blindly following Roa to wherever she was taking me.

"Is this something I have to actually go somewhere

for?" Like, couldn't I just be onboarded over some coffee at home? Not that I had any coffee to offer her.

"Well, the thing is, you're in luck. There's a job fair going on today."

A job fair? Wasn't being a magical girl a job in itself? But there was Roa smiling at me, a smile that said she understood the chaos in my mind, or perhaps the opposite—that she had absolutely no idea what was going on inside my head.

"So all these people are magical girls?" I asked.

"Not really. Some are, but a lot are agents who support them. And even more people who want to be magical girls or agents."

The conference hall wasn't large, but it wasn't small either. I didn't count them, but it looked like there were about a hundred booths. People were lined up outside trying to get in. Roa, a working magical girl, had a VIP pass that let us skip the line. *I guess I'll stick this on the fridge later*, I thought as I sanitized my hands and stroked my entry bracelet.

"The job with the lowest barrier to entry is bounty hunter. I also worked in the hunter guild before I moved to the union."

She pointed to a large booth located near the entrance. It was for the bounty hunters. Some people posed with cardboard cutouts of the more popular hunters. *Fascinating. So magical girls aren't always motivated by selfless ideals like they make it seem on the news.* It was the first time I realized being a magical girl could involve making money, which gave me a strange feeling.

"But, Roa, isn't your ability unrelated to fighting?"

"Believe me, it's harder to find the people on wanted posters than it is to beat them down." Roa smiled and held out a fist. "Besides, I'm very handy in a fight. It's not like I need magic to fight a nonmagic person, convenient as that might be."

I nodded; the confidence and speed with which this fist was presented to me made me think she was onto something.

"Magical girls also make popular bodyguards. The pay is high compared to the difficulty, which means the girls prefer it to bounty hunting. But normally you build experience as a bounty hunter before moving on. You've got to prove yourself on the field first, in other words."

The next booth she pointed out happened to be right

across from the bodyguard agency booth, one that proclaimed to be against the privatization of magical girls. Roa noticed I was looking in that direction and turned me away from them.

"That's a religious organization."

"Are they dangerous?"

"We can't say for certain, but surely making magical girls into gods isn't healthy either. Being a magical girl is like having a rare license or certification. Can you imagine worshipping a lawyer or a florist?"

That made sense. I nodded.

"Aside from the religiousness, their positions aren't that different from the union. They think magical girls should use their power for the community and not just individuals, that kind of thing. Our talents aren't earned through effort, after all."

My nodding slowed to a stop. If we didn't earn talent through effort, didn't that make us different from normal licensed and certified professions . . . ? Just as I was thinking this, the magical girl cram school caught my eye.

"Then what do they teach at that school there?" I asked.

"How to realize your powers and use your abilities, I suppose. I don't really know, actually," Roa said. "There's someone at the union who teaches there. Apparently, they're not the kind of school that tells people becoming a magical girl is a matter of effort to rip girls off. You have to take an entrance test to gauge your potential, and if you aren't up to par, they reject you. Or, if you're really determined to work in this sphere, they encourage you to become an agent."

"Shouldn't I take classes there or something?"

But then I thought of tuition fees. Roa seemed to think I already had the potential to be a great—nay, the greatest—magical girl and that I could potentially do more with my abilities. This time, Roa didn't merely smile but burst into actual laughter.

"Sure, sparrows can teach pigeons and eagles how to fly if they really have no idea how."

I didn't get what was so funny and my feelings were a little hurt. Roa was still wiping away tears as she continued to speak.

"But the Pegasus and dragons have nothing to learn from sparrows."

It sounded like a compliment, but I was still a bit confused about—well, the whole thing. Roa held my hand again and pulled me along.

"Come on. The union is going to have an important announcement shortly."

I let myself be led by the hand to a large presentation screen in the middle of the conference hall. Over the PA, someone announced a union symposium titled A Sustainable Earth and Magical Girls was about to begin. Roa dragged me to the front of the screen and introduced me to some women who seemed to be in union leadership positions. *This is who I was talking about.* Whenever Roa said that, the magical girl I was being introduced to would go, *Oh my!* and give me a little bow, with her hands gathered in front of her. I should've paid more attention to my attire, should've . . . taken a shower, maybe . . . I smiled awkwardly.

The symposium's moderator—I surmised that was her role—went up to the podium.

"We shall now begin the National Trade Union of Magical Girls symposium, A Sustainable Earth and Magical Girls, hosted by the Third Annual Magical Girls Job Fair. To present our keynote, I would like to introduce our union chair, the first magical girl in Korean history—"

Before she could even finish, a door magically appeared onstage. When it opened, a woman wearing a white shirt and black leggings stepped out. The audience applauded. Wow . . . I guess such tricks are possible when one is a magical girl. I clapped along.

Until the moderator, clearly disconcerted, cut in.

"Everyone, this isn't our union chair. This is the Spatial Magical Girl, Choi Heejin."

The applause turned into murmurs. Choi Heejin gestured to the moderator to hand her a microphone. A technician gave her one.

"So sorry. I was trying to get to the greatest concentration of magical girls in one place, and I see I've ended up onstage. Let me make this quick: I need three magical girls to help me catch a terrorist. Peace out."

She held out the microphone and dropped it onto the stage.

How to Fight Like a Magical Girl

The airport was quiet, calm, and almost empty of travelers. The screams of fleeing folks still rang in my ears, making my heart palpitate. Never having been to an airport in my life, I briefly wondered if this was normal. (Were airports always this large? Were there always so many glass walls? Were the signs always in English?) I saw the occasional damaged hunk of equipment, though that probably wasn't due to terrorists but travelers making a run for it.

Choi Heejin hummed as she drew a doorway in the air, stepped inside, and stepped back out of it.

"So, I've talked to the kids who work here, and they tell me almost everyone has been evacuated, but they haven't found a bomb. I think you ladies just need to find the bomb."

"Who are the 'kids' she's referring to?" I asked Roa in a small voice, but it was Heejin who answered.

"The British kids, who else. Who are you, unni?"

"I brought her," said Roa, answering for me, the "sister" in question. "I thought it would be a nice field trip."

Wait, what did Heejin say just before that? Britain? I'd never taken a domestic flight in my life and now I was in England? No wonder all the signs were in English . . .

Roa straightened my shoulders and said, firmly, "Don't worry, I'll take care of you."

Uh, you're a clairvoyant . . . How are you going to protect me in a crisis? But I didn't say this—her eager eyes were too sparkly.

It was Heejin who voiced my concerns in a somewhat more direct manner.

"A field trip?"

"Yes, a field trip."

"Take care of her?"

"Yes, I'm going to take care of her."

Heejin glared while Roa smiled back, the antagonism almost crackling sparks between them. *Isn't anyone curious about how I feel?* I thought, *I just want to get out of here . . . Why does this have to be my first trip overseas?!*

"Unni, aren't you just a clairvoyant?" Heejin asked.

"I am," Roa said.

"Does this look like some kind of a joke to you?"

"Nope."

Roa's answers were almost curt. Heejin's hackles rose, then smoothed over.

"A field trip when thousands of lives could be on the— fine. It's my fault for grabbing whoever I could to get the job done."

You yourself were humming just a second ago! I don't want to be here either!

But Heejin threw her hands up in defeat. "Y'know what, whatever, we don't have time for this. Let's split up. A few planes can't take off right now because of the terrorists, okay? I'm going to go evacuate them. You unnis can go find the bomb, and take care of any lingering terrorists. Regroup soon. Bye!"

She disappeared, then reappeared with two electric golf carts and disappeared again. Roa explained that they used golf carts in airports too.

So, there I was with Roa and two magical girls I had never met before. The one in the sundress and sunglasses pushed her shades to the top of her head and said, "I think

I'll work on my own, thanks. If something comes up, I'll let you know. See ya."

I learned later she was the Magical Girl of Scent, and her name was Cha Minhwa. Scent . . . If that was your superpower, shouldn't that make you less eager to go around on your own? But Roa explained that she used scents that paralyzed or made you hallucinate, which meant it was better for her to work at a distance from other magical girls.

"We should get going too."

Roa and the other remaining magical girl sat in the front of the golf cart Minhwa didn't take, while I sat in the back. I had a feeling that this magical girl would need to have some kind of amazing superpower for a clairvoyant and me to survive this mission, but the thing about her was . . . Well, she was very short. Maybe she was even a dwarf. Her head barely reached Roa's shoulders. For a while we rode through the airport, not talking to each other. *I guess she's a woman of few words.* Not that I was being particularly chatty myself. I felt so awkward that I almost hoped we'd run into these terrorists already to break the silence.

"You do know that every magical girl has a different ability?"

Of course, it was Roa who broke the silence. I didn't feel like speaking for some reason, so I answered with a nod. But Roa couldn't even see me because she had to keep her eyes on the road.

"Everyone's ability on a case-by-case basis seems slight. And some have abilities that actually are minor. But depending on how you use your ability, results will differ."

Roa stopped the cart. I could see the runway through the large windows. *I guess we really are in another country. It must be around three or four in Korea, but it's almost morning here.* Was Korea nine hours ahead of the UK? I tried to recall the world time clock in Grandfather's store. The planes standing in rows far and near looked so much like toys that it almost seemed like we weren't in a terrorist situation.

"It's true being clairvoyant isn't very useful in a fight."

Roa's words brought me back to the present. She must have a lot to say. Maybe Heejin had rattled her a bit.

"But the ability to know when and where one must be is important. I can see this situation playing out in a couple of ways. In a few cases, we fail to suppress the terrorists; in a few, we partially succeed; and in one case, we're very successful. Only I can see these outcomes—I use the Ahroamirror when I need to show any of them to other people."

So that's what that mirror was for. I was only half listening to her, still mesmerized by the sight outside.

The short magical girl piped up, "How far are we from the likelihood of complete success?"

"This time around, the likelihood of complete success and complete failure are about the same." Roa said.

"Excuse me . . ."

I knew they were discussing something important, but I couldn't not butt in. I could see it clear as day, since I was staring outside the windows and all. One of the airplanes was heading in this direction—despite my inexperience with airplanes and airports, I was *pretty sure* that plane wasn't supposed to head straight toward us.

"Yes, now," said Roa, nodding to the short magical girl.

Thanks to the glass, the surrounding silence made the plane's approach even more surreal, as it now very much did not look like a toy plane.

The short magical girl leaped off the cart. A shadow suddenly fell over us and the window wall shattered with the most spectacular noise.

Even as I witnessed it with my own eyes, I couldn't believe it.

A fist as large as the cart we'd been riding in had smashed through the windows. A fist attached to the person I had, until recently, referred to as the "short magical girl." She hopped out of the hole she'd made in the glass and expanded her whole body to be proportional to her enlarged fist; the still-advancing airplane looked like a toy in comparison.

The large magical girl picked up the plane like it weighed nothing and flung it into the air—"Whoopsies"—as though she was letting go of a dragonfly. Roa and I threw our heads back like how the crowd at a baseball game watches a home run ball disappear into the horizon. Somewhere, in the distance, the plane exploded.

I learned later from the news that the airport we'd been in was Heathrow, Heejin had helped hundreds of travelers evacuate, and Cha Minhwa had a decisive role in suppressing the terrorists. The large magical girl's name was Ahn Subin, and as the Magical Girl of Growth, she could become a giant at will. The plane she had picked up had been filled with explosives, and if they had gone off in her possession, she would've lost an entire arm.

Also, the British government gave the magical girls of Korea commemorative plaques and a cash reward!

Not that I had done anything, but Roa insisted we needed to split the reward, which was why I found myself at the union office. Roa brought me to the offices with her in a taxi and held my hand again.

"How do you feel?" she asked.

"A little unsettled. I don't know if I should accept the money."

Because the money was apportioned according to merit, I wasn't getting much to begin with, but the sum was still quite generous.

"Of course you should accept it. If it weren't for the fact that it was a field trip, I wouldn't have even gone, and if I hadn't gone, Subin wouldn't have thrown the plane at the right time and place. The damage to the airport would've been extensive, even if there wouldn't have been any casualties."

On the other hand, I also needed the money. I wanted to ask Roa if she knew what a revolving balance was, but I stopped myself. Instead, I said: "I do feel a little like Cinderella. Maybe the magic will wear off when I get home."

We arrived at a large and old building in the Jongno District. It looked more appropriate for old men playing Go than a union for magical girls. Roa held open a glass door for me and said, "I bet you want to learn what your powers are already."

"So, uh, about that," I said as we mounted some decidedly unmagical stairs. "What exactly do I have to do to become a magical girl?"

What's Precious to a Magical Girl

They say a person's memory generally activates at around four or five. Some remember before that, but apparently those are made-up memories. *When you were little, you could eat very hot food. Look at this photo, you were always dragging around a yellow blanket.* People listen to stories like that and make up memories. When the comments are specific enough, the imagination can produce false memories. Like fearlessly biting down on a spoon hot from the pot, or the texture of a yellow blanket that has long been lost. But I don't know if it's right to call them false. Memories are subjective, after all. The reason we're able to recall vivid details after hearing a brief comment or seeing a single picture must be because a very similar memory is living somewhere inside our brains. How can we call such things fake?

I have a memory like that. I am sitting on Grandfather's lap, staring at his watch. I'm two? Three? Maybe I was younger than that. His watch was an old model of an expensive brand; it glinted with gold. *Oh, look, she already wants to see his watch! Hahaha!* I can hear the adults laughing. Which is odd, because I would not have been of an age to understand adults.

There's a photo of this scene. Whether I created a fake memory from this photo, or whether it's proof of my memory's veracity . . . I don't know. The objective facts are thus: There's a baby sitting on Grandfather's lap. Because this is really a baby photo, Grandfather is only visible below his shoulders. He wears a gold watch on his wrist. The baby is now twenty-nine years old, and she owned that watch until recently. Which is how she knows the adult in the photograph, even if we can't see his face, is her grandfather.

"Is this your most prized possession?"

"There aren't that many photos of me as a child. It's the thing associated with my oldest memory, so I think it's safe to say it is."

Roa had asked me to bring my most precious belonging; she said it was needed. I had wondered what the union headquarters would do with my most prized possession, and now that Roa was asking, I was almost embarrassed about it even though I knew Roa hadn't been mocking me when she asked.

"You must've loved your grandfather very much."

This was the chairperson of the union speaking, Yeon Liji. Chairperson Yeon was very tall and had sorrowful eyes, and it felt a little odd to call her a magical girl, seeing as she was more or less a granny. *So this is her, the first magical girl in Korean history.*

"How did you know it was my grandfather?" I asked.

She couldn't see his face, so it would've been safer to assume the man was my father, but she had astonishingly guessed correctly on the first try. The chairperson smiled a little cryptically and said, "I just knew. So, let me ask you the same question, is this your most prized possession?"

"Oh—and this . . ." I mumbled as I brought out the first watch Grandfather had ever given me.

When I was very young, or when my real and false memories overlapped with each other, I lived with Grandfather—it was just the two of us—and I learned how to tell time long before other kids my age did. Which was why Grandfather thought I was some kind of genius. I guess telling time is the kind of thing diffi-cult enough to be taught in a textbook, so being able to do it before kindergarten age seemed like a big deal. But seeing as I had trouble reading and writing until I was ten, I was by no means a genius. I just liked watches.

When I was six or seven, Grandfather asked me to pick out whatever watch in his store that I liked the best. Be-lieving I was a genius, he was determined to entice me with the best watches he had, but I shook my head at all of them and ended up grabbing a sporty electronic watch with a light blue strap. Because . . . Hello Kitty was on it. I remember Grandfather laughing. He might've been a lit-tle disappointed, but I laughed along with him. I gripped the watch—which has zero resale value, by the way—inside my fist.

It was such a pathetic little thing that I was worried the chairperson would also laugh, but with seeming rever-ence, she gently picked it up.

"Would you mind terribly if this item disappeared?"

"Disappeared?"

"We're going to use your most precious memory to create a talisman for you. I suppose the word I'm looking for isn't 'disappear' but 'transfigure.'"

"Is a talisman really necessary?"

Just a moment ago, I'd been sheepish about the watch looking small and pathetic, but the prospect of it disappearing filled me with dread.

"You don't really need a talisman, but . . . how do I explain this . . ."

She glanced at Roa, and Roa took out her Ahroamirror and stood up from her seat. Then . . .

"I want to know what happens next! Will we all be happy tomorrow? I shall answer! Clairvoyant Magical Girl Ah Roa, transform!"

Light arched out from the Ahroamirror, and the white dress Roa was wearing turned into a luminescent robe that refracted with a rainbow shimmer. So this was a magical girl transformation! Wait—did that mean that white dress she wore all the time was just . . . her regular clothes?

Roa put a hand on her hip. "You've seen me in action, so you know we don't need to transform if we want to use our powers. But if you have a talisman, you can transform, and once you do that, you can acclimate to your powers more easily."

"Oh, I see . . . so if magical girls are bicycles, are talismans training wheels?"

"More like a magical girl is a bike rider and her ability is the bike itself," answered the chairperson with a smile. "There are many magical girls out there who don't have talismans, which means they can't transform. Some don't even need to use their talismans, since manifesting their power comes so naturally to them. Like Little Miss Clairvoyant, over here. And then there are those who come to me later for talismans because they want to make better use of their powers, and those I create a talisman for before they even realize their powers—those magical girls are in a rush."

Like me.

"In a rush?" I asked.

The chairperson and Roa looked at each other. I couldn't help thinking they were conspiring, or at least holding something back from me.

Roa said, "We have come to a consensus that . . . the end of the world is near."

"By 'we,' we mean magical girls around the world, not just Korea." The chairperson's voice was solemn.

"Once the alarm was raised, in global solidarity, magical girls put stopping the apocalypse as our highest priority."

"Which is why it was so important for us to find out

who the Magical Girl of Time was. She's our key to the world beyond this crisis."

I frantically waved my hands at them.

"Wait a minute, did you say apocalypse? Like there's going to be some demon or alien coming to destroy us? Or a huge war? And magical girls already know about this?"

"No, *everyone* knows about it. Absolutely everyone. The real crisis, the real apocalypse, is climate change." The chairperson's warm gaze suddenly turned fearsome. "The world will not end because of some demon or alien. At least, not anytime soon. But climate change is an actual disaster that will destroy civilization as we know it."

Then again, that day when we ended up at Heathrow— wasn't there a lot of talk about sustainability or something? What was the title of that symposium again . . . I'd missed it because of my little field trip, but it had something to do with the environment. I was pretty sure it didn't have anything to do with recycling.

"The Magical Girl of Time has a very important role," the chairperson continued. "We have some strategies in mind. When the Magical Girl of Time stops Earth's clock, magical girls around the world shall work together to dismantle any facility that compromises sustainability to let

Earth recover its glaciers . . . And then there's our last resort."

Her throat seemed to close, and Roa took over.

"We have a backup plan in case we need to restart Earth. And it's something only the Magical Girl of Time can pull off."

"But wouldn't that just be a self-inflicted apocalypse? A more directly self-inflicted one, I mean."

"That's why it's our last resort."

Chills ran down my arms. To become a Magical Girl of Time and use the powers of time at will meant holding the fate of the universe in my hands. These people were trying to use that power to save the world.

"We'll only exercise that option when all others have been exhausted, of course. And I assure you that the most important part of this plan is whether the Magical Girl of Time is willing to implement it."

"All right." I nodded. "I guess I'll take a talisman then. Please."

It heartened me to see Roa and the chairperson look so joyful. Beyond feeling compelled by the idea I could in fact become someone important—and selfishly thinking about how I could make a nice living off of this—I was feeling something close to, if I may be so bold, a real calling. *All right*, I thought, *let's try this magical girl thing . . .*

"Now, give me your prized possession," the chairperson said.

"You're going to make it yourself?"

"Of course. I'm the Magical Girl of Making. I made these oven mitts myself. There isn't a single talisman owned by a Korean magical girl out there that hasn't come from these mitts."

"Oh . . . Then I'm in your hands."

I gave her the photograph and watch; I had a feeling that either one would not be enough. It didn't feel like I was losing them. They weren't expensive objects, and while the memories they held made them special, there was something wonderful about the fact that their specialness would make me into a magical girl. It made them even more special, if that makes sense.

"Good choices. The more your heart is in the object, the more effective the talisman is."

With her left hand, the chairperson held my right, in which I held the photo and watch, then covered our cupped hands with her right. With my hand wrapped in her pair of oven mitts, she closed her eyes. The faintly glowing mittens slowly brightened as rays of rainbow light emitted from between her gloves. Something warm squirmed inside my hand, making my heart pound.

"The talisman will appear as an object that is very close to your heart. Put your whole heart into them."

The rainbow light intensified and I could feel something taking physical shape. I could keep my fist closed no longer, and when I opened it, a ball of light squeezed out from between the chairperson's oven mitts.

Grandfather, I'm about to become a magical girl. How incredible . . . It's really happening. I'm becoming a magical girl.

The chairperson finally started bringing her hands apart little by little, and the ball of light began fading into a rectangle that was spinning on one of its corners. Roa and I leaned in toward it, our shoulders touching. I was so close to it that if it were made of fire, the tip of my nose would've burned off.

"What . . . what is it?" Roa asked in wonder.

As it continued to take form, the spinning started to slow, but even before it stopped, I knew what it was.

"I think . . . it's a credit card."

"A credit card?" Roa tilted her head, perplexed.

The object that was now floating in the air was, unmistakably, a credit card. With a magnetic strip on one side and my name embossed on the other, but no bank name or anything . . . just a black credit card.

I'm sure we were all wondering why a magical girl's talisman would take the form of a credit card, but none of us dared to ask.

Transforming into the Magical Girl of Time

The credit-card-shaped magical talisman lightly landed in the palm of my hand. Roa, the chairperson, and I stared down at it for a good while without saying a word.

"How . . ." The chairperson seemed to be choosing her next words carefully. ". . . special." She smiled a winning smile.

Not a bad thing to say really—it was a good thing if you gave it some thought—but it's like when you see a puppy or a baby that's not cute and you can't bear to lie, so you say things like, "He looks so strong," or "What a clever-looking boy." It was embarrassing, to say the least, that my heart's truest form was . . . a credit card. Way to tell the whole world that a corner of my mind is forever colonized by the thought of my credit card debt.

But more so than that, what did a credit card have to do

with time? Time is money? Therefore, money is time? The more time that passes, the bigger your debt is? You could come up with any number of meanings, but surely that couldn't be the symbol of a whole magical girl. It seemed immoral somehow.

The chairperson took off her mitts and said, "You won't be able to transform at will for a while. That's just how it works—no need to be distressed or embarrassed about it. Ask Roa for help. And think of a good chant for your transformation spell. I recommend practicing where it's bright and there's lots of room. You . . . might find it hard to keep your energy under control."

I pressed down hard on the tears that threatened and cleared my throat.

"Thank you, ma'am."

The chairperson smiled warmly again.

"Young lady, you are destined to become a great magical girl. I wish you luck."

We left her to spritzing the orchids in her office and exited the building.

Roa took me to a wide park near the Han River. It was the kind of space the chairperson had recommended, but it was embarrassing because quite a few people were playing ball around us. Roa kept pushing me to transform, not understanding my mortification, and I kept hesitating until finally we were at a weird spot in the park between the football field and the parking lot. I took out my talisman. A bit strange, this little talisman, but it was clearly made from my own being, and undoubtedly something I needed to keep with me always.

"What if I lose it?" I asked.

Roa shook her head firmly.

"You can't. It contains a part of you. Even if you drop it somewhere, it will always make its way back to you." She clapped her hands. "Come on! Let's practice!"

"You're acting like such a tiger mom all of a sudden."

"A tiger? Sweetie, I can turn into the devil himself if it means getting results."

Roa was so adamant that I felt intimidated, but I have to admit it was motivating too. I glanced around a bit, holding my credit card aloft like a soccer referee handing out a yellow card, and whispered, "Okay . . . Magical Girl of Time . . . transform?"

Nothing happened.

It was hot outside, but I was sweating not from the heat but from embarrassment.

Roa shouted, "Try harder! Imagine the kind of magical girl you want to be!"

The kind of magical girl I wanted to be. *What kind do I want to be? How do I think that up?* I closed my eyes and imagined myself wearing the type of clothes Roa was wearing. It was so hilarious that I almost giggled. I shouted again, "Magical Girl of Time, transform?"

I thought I'd done all right, but Roa was not an easy teacher.

"Why do you keep putting a question mark at the end? Are you asking a question? Use an exclamation point this time!"

"Magical Girl of Time . . . transform!"

"A comma instead of an ellipsis this time!"

"Magical Girl of Time, transform!"

A light surrounded my talisman and then . . . stopped.

"Look, it's happening! You must be some kind of genius! We might even finish this today!"

Roa clapped her hands as she showered me with praise. I was amazed myself. My talisman . . . my hands . . . magic was coming from them! Even if I didn't succeed in transforming or awakening my powers. Bashfully, I scratched my head with my talisman until my eyes met

Roa's frown. I lowered my hand, though her eyes were still sparkling.

"So, shall we try a specific chant?" Roa asked.

"Wasn't what I just said a chant?"

"Only in the strictest sense, but we need something more. How do I put this . . . What you just did was like striking two stones together to start a fire. Imagining the specific kind of magical girl you want to be is like igniting a chant with a lighter."

"How am I supposed to 'light up' a chant?"

"You have to come up with it yourself."

Roa was staring at me wide-eyed as if I'd asked her something weird. *Are you telling me that I have to come up with something that embarrassing on my own?* I thought. *I can't just wave my talisman over my head and have the chant magically come to me?*

"Just think of it as a way of introducing yourself," Roa said. "You can't introduce yourself by shouting out your name and leaving it at that. Say who you are, what you do, what you hope to do, those sorts of things—pretend like you're at a job interview and the job is being a magical girl . . ."

But . . . I can't even introduce myself as a normal person, much less a magical girl. And who cares where I live, or how old I am, or anything else you'd introduce yourself with? Am I really supposed to say, "Transform into the Magical Girl of Time who lives in Mapo and is twenty-nine years old"?!

"The past, the present, the future . . . magic crawl of time, transform."

My mumbling chant made my talisman react again. Roa leaped to her feet.

"Look at that! It worked a bit better, right?"

"Yeah . . . I think it's making up the chant itself that's the hard part."

"Do you want to crib off my chant?"

"How did it go again?"

"'I want to know what happens next! Will we all be happy tomorrow? I shall answer! Clairvoyant Magical Girl Ah Roa, transform!'"

Roa spoke her transformation spell very quickly. It really suited her, a beautiful chant that completely encapsulated her abilities as a magical girl. *So Roa came up with this herself?* I closed my eyes, held my credit card with both hands, placed it over my chest, and breathed deeply.

Pretend like you're talking to someone. Like you're introducing yourself to someone as a magical girl. Like you're expressing your very existence so someone else would understand. But more than anything else . . . like you're expressing it to yourself.

"Flowing everywhere equally . . ."

I imagined the world time clock in my grandfather's shop.

". . . never stopping nor retreating . . ."

The next image that came to mind was a stopped watch that suddenly started ticking away the seconds again when I replaced the battery.

". . . that which is older and stronger than all else—I call upon the powers of time."

My heart began to beat.

"Magical Girl of Time, transform."

A most refreshing feeling swirled around me, like very sparkly blood was circulating inside of me (or something, but it really felt like that). I also felt a slight floating sensation as well.

I slowly opened my eyes.

Had I succeeded?

The first thing I saw was Roa's eyes, wide as saucers. I checked my limbs and clothes, looking for changes. My clothes were the same, and my feet were still on the ground. But . . . something was different about it all. Like something was really changing, really happening.

"That felt amazing!" I shouted despite myself. "Like . . . this is it! I think I just need to try a tiny bit harder."

Unlike me, who was almost floating off into the air with excitement, Roa had no reaction. She just stared into space, her eyes still saucers.

"What's wrong?"

Why hadn't I picked up on it sooner? If what I'd done had truly been a sign of success, Roa would've been even happier than I was. But she kept gazing at some invisible point in the sky, which at first disappointed me and then began to scare me.

"Roa, what's . . ."

Roa put her hands on her head and sat down where she was. I was at a distance from her in case my transformation unleashed some potent energy; by the time I made it over to her and held out my hand, Roa was . . . crying. Tears ran down her suddenly pale face.

"My prediction was wrong."

She got up without taking my hand.

"I mean, that must happen from time to time," I said, "but why the tears . . . ?"

Embarrassed that my hand had been left hanging, I

clasped it myself. Seeing Roa, who was usually so upbeat and chipper, reduced to tears made me want to cry too.

Roa shook her head.

"My predictions have never been wrong."

I felt my heart drop into my stomach.

Something is really, really off.

This wasn't a strange feeling for me. In fact, when it came to my life, things felt off more often than not. Which was why, despite my distress, I had a feeling about what Roa was going to say next.

Roa cried as she spoke. "The Magical Girl of Time has just awakened her powers for the first time."

My heart found an even deeper level in the pit of my stomach. Roa buried her face in her hands and sat down—no, collapsed—again.

"And she's . . . she's not you."

Letter from a Magical Girl

Would it have helped had I been more serious?

If I'd concentrated more, or were more talented, if I'd awakened my powers just ten, five, or even just one second faster, would Roa's prediction have come true?

"I'm so sorry."

I was thinking I should apologize, but here was Roa apologizing to me instead.

She rubbed her temples as if she had a headache.

"I'm really, really sorry."

She got up and fled the scene. So quickly that I wondered if she wasn't the Clairvoyant Magical Girl but the Magical Girl of Speed.

I stood there as if there was something left for me to

do. Roa shrank into the distance until she disappeared. Until the shadows on the edge of the park came to cover my head.

Until staring at the black credit card in my hand made me feel ashamed of myself.

On the way home, I dropped by a convenience store and picked up a bottle of water; I tried to see if I could buy something with my card, but of course, it didn't work.

It was two days later when I found a white envelope wedged under my door. There was no name on it, and despite its location, the envelope remained a pristine white, which gave me a hint as to whom the letter was from.

The stationery was decorated with a lace border, and this was what was written at the top:

Hello, it's Ah Roa.

Of course.

I felt relieved but also a little bit resentful. Glad as I was that I wasn't completely abandoned by her, I couldn't help but feel slighted by this whole situation.

I'm really sorry for leaving the way I did yesterday. No matter what I felt like at the time, that was just very rude of me.

Yesterday. Did that mean it had been more than a day since she left the letter there? After coming home that day, I'd spent my time lying in bed doing nothing, unaware of any letters arriving.

But would it have made a difference if I had known? Would I have asked her in, to talk? Me?

There are so many things I want to say to you, but since I'm feeling shy, I figured I'd write to you instead, but now that I'm writing to you, I don't know where to begin.

First, I want to tell you how happy I was when I met you.

You have no idea how long we've waited for the advent of the Magical Girl of Time. The union and every magical girl around the globe have all waited for her in solidarity, but no one wanted her to appear more than me. The Clairvoyant Magical Girl should be able to say anything with conviction, but this I can say with more conviction than anything else. No one waited harder for the Magical Girl of Time than I did.

Because a prediction is, of course, a truth about the future.

And also, the act of turning the present into the past.

My work has a lot to do with the power of time, and depending on the perspective, the Clairvoyant Magical Girl would be considered a sidekick to the Magical Girl of Time. At least, that's what I believe.

We magical girls with invisible powers are a little insecure. Some more than others, of course. We're a bit looked down on by the other magical girls, and so we're a little less trusting of our own powers. I know this very well, my powers being what they are. My powers seem like nothing until my predictions come true. Which was why I wanted more than anyone else for the Magical Girl of Time to be found. She would make my powers whole.

Predictions have no power on their own, but if someone should appear who has the power to make those predictions come true, we could do the most spectacular things together. Finding her became my ultimate mission.

And I found you.

I felt more confused as I read on. It looked like Roa was trying to say how happy she was to have met me, but the more she explained how she had longed for the Magical Girl of Time to appear, the more sorry I felt that she wasn't me.

Maybe I was too arrogant. Like I said, I've never made a wrong prediction.

Again, it was important that the person I ended up finding was you. The fact that my clairvoyance had never let me down, the hope that my sometimes pathetic-seeming power would be enhanced by the Magical Girl of Time—all of this made me think of you. You, out of everyone else in the world.

So . . . I know I seemed very upset yesterday and that I made some mistakes, but I don't think finding you was a mistake. I don't have even the tiniest doubt about it.

But I do owe you an apology, I've realized.

You must've been confused. Maybe even hated me. I understand if that's the case. If I'd been in your position, I would've hated the Clairvoyant Magical Girl too.

Hate Roa? Never. Sure, I felt resentment but not at all toward her. I resented myself.

Because I'd thought I finally found what I was meant to do in this world. That not only was I useful but essential. I hadn't for a second doubted I was the Magical Girl of Time.

It wasn't Roa who had ruined everything—it was me.

I even thought it was my bad luck that ruined Roa's prediction, not any failure on her part.

But I had a feeling that Roa already knew all of these thoughts running through my head.

If you're blaming yourself, please don't. It's my fault that I didn't understand my own prediction properly.

There's a reason the Ahroamirror showed me your face. It's proof that you have the power of magic too. The fact that we could even make a talisman, and that it responded to your transformation chant is all because you are a true magical girl. It may have been my mistake to name you as the Magical Girl of Time, but according to the Ahroamirror, we were meant to meet. I have no doubt about that. It's funny how being a clairvoyant means you also believe ardently in things like destiny and fate. We share a destiny that is too powerful to ignore. I hope you believe in it too.

Now that we know the Magical Girl of Time, somewhere, has awakened her powers, our first priority is to track her down. Because I need to find her as quickly as possible to ask for her help in saving the world, I'm very sorry to say that it will be difficult for us to meet in the interim.

But of all the magical girls I have found, you will always be the most important one to me. My beliefs about the Magical Girl of Time notwithstanding. This was truly something I did not—no, could not have predicted.

Can you understand how disconcerting it is for the Clairvoyant Magical Girl to be met with an unanticipated event? But you know . . . I kind of like this feeling. I don't know why, but I do.

I started writing this to apologize, but why have I ended up making a confession?

I'll come see you as soon as I'm done here. Please promise me you'll invite me in.

From, Ah Roa

Roa's handwriting was small and rounded, making her vowels a bit confusing and the rounder letters almost interchangeable. I read and reread her bad handwriting that looked embroidered on the pretty stationery. I cried a little, and then, like I've been doing for the past two days, lay on my back and stared up at the ceiling.

I laid her letter neatly by my pillow.

The Clairvoyant Magical Girl and I

A week passed in the blink of an eye. Was it because the Magical Girl of Time had appeared? I had gotten into the habit of thinking that she was at the root of everything that happened in my life. When my instant ramyun didn't cook as quickly as I'd expected it to and the noodles ended up crunchy, or the expensive perm I got last year turned completely straight that week, or not seeing Roa made time slip by faster than I'd thought it would—everything felt like it was because of the Magical Girl of Time. I knew a great and powerful person like that wouldn't spend so much energy messing around with stupid little me, but whenever I became aware of the passage of time, I couldn't help but think that was the case.

Had I come to hate the Magical Girl of Time? Someone

I had never met or even knew the face of? Someone who had never harmed me in my life?

Someone who probably didn't even know I existed?

It had been about two days since I finally gathered up my wits and looked for another part-time job. Roa did say that just because I wasn't the Magical Girl of Time, it didn't mean I wasn't a magical girl at all. But I'd lost my incentive to awaken my powers quickly, and there was also no more guarantee that I would become the greatest—or even simply a great—magical girl. Which meant I better ready myself for living an ordinary life. To pay off my god-damn credit card debt and do something about my perm that'd given up on life.

Afraid of what my metro card would charge me at the end of the month, I first looked for workplaces that were within walking distance. Restaurants, convenience stores, internet cafés, café cafés, billiard halls, offices, clothing stores, accessory stores—Why were there no jewelry or watch stores looking for people nowadays?—going down the list of places I could walk to within an hour, then to places twenty to thirty minutes away by bus, then going all the way to Gyeonggi Province before getting ahold of myself.

I looked at a lot of places but only a fraction of them looked like they'd give me the time of day. *Help wanted. Nearby residents preferred. College graduate and up. Twenty to twenty-four years old.* These words made me feel rejected right off the bat, crushing me before I could hastily click the back button on my browser. And what the hell were these "modern bars" and "talking bars" that were always looking for people? The hours were flexible, and they claimed beginners could make a good chunk of money if they wanted to, and there was a "modern bar" that was within walking distance, which made me look very closely at the ad. But then, when I looked up, my eyes happened to fall on Roa's business card, which made me quickly click the back button again. (I had no idea what went on in those bars, but I felt embarrassed for some reason.) I could hear Grandfather clucking his tongue. I could almost hear him refer to himself in the third person, just the way he did whenever he wanted to criticize me: *What a great job your grandfather must think you're doing.*

Calls came from a convenience store fifteen minutes away and an internet café twenty minutes away. The café asked if I had my health insurance card and I said I didn't; they didn't reply. The convenience store said, contrary to what they mentioned in their ad, that they only had week-end slots left but if I was okay with that I should come for an interview. Well, it was in a residential area, so it looked okay—at least it wasn't near a college or a nightlife district. And the internet café might follow up and offer me a weekday job . . .

I did my best to look presentable for the convenience store interview, but the only question they asked me was if I could start right away. When I said I could begin that very weekend, the manager told me about the paperwork I needed to prepare for them by then and told me a long story about how she didn't really want to hire anyone for the weekends, but her father was not doing well and needed her support, which was why she had no choice but to hire me.

"It's a lot of moving around boxes, so I was hoping to hire a man. But you look very capable for a young lady, so let's see how you do."

"My own grandfather was sick for a long time, I really do sympathize . . ."

My saying this prompted her to go on another long story about her father. *See*, she said, *I knew you were a nice, capable young person,* which made it impossible for me to say no to her. I managed to get out of there well after the sun had set. I had been asked just one question during our entire interview!

What did it mean to be nice and capable? Did it mean I couldn't say no to things? That was just me on the outside; on the inside I wasn't thinking very nice thoughts. At first, yes, the manager's story really did get me thinking about Grandfather, but it wasn't like it'd made me that sad; we'd only just met.

I was about halfway home when something cool hit the top of my head. Then I was hit on the cheek, the shoulder—rain. A squall, and a wet one. *Dammit . . . if I hadn't had to listen to that manager's life story, I would be home by now. And it wouldn't have mattered if it rained or snowed or what.*

Wondering if there was a point to running, I raised my arm to cover my head, but there was no rain falling on my arm. I looked up to see a big umbrella covering me.

"Did you miss me?"

Only the Clairvoyant Magical Girl would say such a thing. How else could she have known I was here without ever asking me, shielding me from rain that had even eluded the weather report? But the question was also un-becoming of the Clairvoyant Magical Girl.

I turned to Roa and said, "Of course."

Did you? I wanted to ask, but I knew I would burst into tears if I did. We stood like that in the rain for a moment, sharing her umbrella, trying to find the words to say to each other.

Roa, like always, clasped my hand.

"How have you been?"

"Roa, you know that I know that you know."

She smiled. "I don't read minds or engage in psychometry; I just predict things. I can't know absolutely everything. Just fragments about things I really concentrate on."

Considering that Roa usually spoke of her abilities with great pride, this admission seemed all the more sincere to me. "Then that means you haven't been concentrating on me at all."

My joke only put a sad expression on her face.

"Actually, I concentrated on you a lot. Which distracted me, making me less able to predict things."

"I'm sorry," I said.

"Why? What for?"

"For getting into your head?"

Roa's frown dispersed with a laugh.

"Why on earth are you apologizing for getting into my head?"

"I have no idea." My silly answer made her laugh again, making me feel even sillier. "You really didn't predict how I'd feel?"

She nodded, her eyes still filled with amusement. Shyly, I dropped my gaze to the ground as we walked on. The sound of the rain pattering on Roa's big, white umbrella and our two sets of feet plodding through the puddles created a kind of pleasant cacophony for a while.

"These past few—"

"Have you found—"

Good grief. I'd thought this kind of situation happened only in manhwa or dramas. Relieved to have thought of a question, I was about to ask it when Roa began asking a question of her own. Our gazes met—*zing*—like two sabers fencing, and we stepped away from each other, opening and closing our mouths in sync.

I mean, of course I'd make such a mistake, but Roa?

Maybe Roa had said something deliberately to stop me from asking. Which meant it was probably better for me not to ask it. I had just wanted to know if she and the union had made any progress finding the real Magical Girl of Time . . . Maybe this was her way of warning me that it was probably best for a nobody like me not to meddle in such important affairs.

"I know what you were going to ask. I'll explain later."

So I was right.

"Ask your question first, Roa."

"There was something more pressing I wanted to tell you."

My heart started beating fast. What could possibly be more important at this point in history than finding the Magical Girl of Time? And didn't the fact that she had come to find me to talk about it prove that it had something to do with me?

Another part of me was going, *Fool me once shame on you, fool me twice shame on me*, but I couldn't help thinking, *Maybe this time it's real, maybe I'm just as important as the Magical Girl of Time—or even more important*. My heart continued to pound.

"I've thought long and hard about it. About why the Ahroamirror showed me your face so clearly."

Hoping Roa wouldn't hear me nervously swallow, I nodded.

"I don't claim to know all the different functions of the Ahroamirror. It's not like there's an instructional manual for it. But like all talismans, the Ahroamirror responds to the imagination of the user."

Roa suddenly stopped in her tracks and looked me in the eye.

"Remember when I told you I would protect you?"

She'd said that? *Oh wait, at Heathrow.* I nodded, and Roa grabbed both of my hands.

"That's just it," she said.

"Just what?"

"The protecting you part."

Excuse me? I peered at her through narrowed eyes as she swung our joined hands from side to side.

"You're someone I need to protect. You're not the most important magical girl in the world, you are the most important girl in the world—to me."

When did the rain stop . . . ?

Realizing I was dry despite Roa having let go of her umbrella, I looked up. It was still raining, but the umbrella was floating in the air on its own, protecting us from the downpour.

"It was you! You were my destiny the whole time!"

Roa's voice, filled with conviction, seemed to be coming from somewhere in the distance.

Awkward Even for a Magical Girl

Roa let go of my hands—my complicated feelings must've shown up on my face.

"I don't expect things to change all of a sudden or anything. I apologize if using a word like 'destiny' made you feel uncomfortable."

"It's . . ."

It's not that, I wanted to say, but the traffic jam inside my head made it impossible to know what *it* was or wasn't.

"But I am the Clairvoyant Magical Girl, after all. If I felt it wouldn't work out, I wouldn't have even mentioned it."

Setting what she was actually saying aside, her firm— exuberant, really—way of saying it made me think that everything was going to work out all right. *I don't know for sure yet, but I like you too, Roa. Maybe not in the same way as you like me, but I want you to always be by my side. I have no idea how you managed to like me, but well, if that's how you feel . . .*

"Thank you."

My answer made Roa clench her hands into fists.

"You'll see! Before long, you'll be saying you like me too."

Well, if the Clairvoyant Magical Girl thinks so, then it must be true, I thought as I took her hand. The floating umbrella came down and landed in Roa's other hand. It was much later when I realized that was the very first time I had reached out to take her hand, rather than the other way around.

"So who was the real Magical Girl of Time?"

I thought this would be an easier question for Roa to answer than whether she had succeeded in making contact with her. Roa glanced at me sideways before giving a knowing smile, as if she understood I was trying to make things less difficult.

"Someone who would be very frightening if she wasn't going to be on our side."

Aha, she's met her. I'm guessing she's probably younger than me? She must be so powerful she doesn't even need a talisman to realize her powers.

"Our side?"

"I hope so," she said.

"Are you saying she isn't?"

"She's not on anyone's side at the moment. But judging by her refusal to join our union and some other issues that have come up, perhaps she's . . ."

Roa became lost in thought, her words trailing off.

"The thing is," she continued, "usually there's an incident that leads to a magical girl coming into her powers. We call them triggers. For example, maybe the only student at a small country school ends up becoming a magical girl of making because she really wanted to 'make a friend,' or a girl loses her parents to a car accident, wishes she could predict accidents, and becomes a clairvoyant magical girl . . . That sort of thing."

Was she talking about herself? I gripped her hand a little harder. *If that really is your story, you and I have much more in common than I thought. Maybe we really are destined for each other.*

"How did the Magical Girl of Time realize her powers?" I asked.

"When do you think people normally hope for time to stop in its tracks?"

"Well . . . maybe when they're really happy?"

Roa came to a stop, turning to look at me with an arched eyebrow.

"And why is that?"

"I don't know . . . You might want time to stop when you're in so much pain or have been through something awful, but as soon as time starts back up, you'll have to go through it all over again. I think in those cases it would be better to turn back time instead to give yourself a chance to make different choices. If you had the means to go back in time and not just to start or stop time, I mean. But if you're feeling happy, I think you would make the moment last longer."

Roa seemed lost in thought again, her head slightly bowed as we resumed walking.

"Whereas the Magical Girl of Time seems to have used her power to keep moving forward," she said.

No wonder she looked surprised just now; my thought had been the opposite of what the Magical Girl of Time had thought. Now that I had nothing to do with that particular magical girl, I immediately stopped caring about the look of surprise on Roa's face. (Of course, if this was true and I really didn't care, I wouldn't have been having this thought in the first place.)

"In a very painful moment, she wished time would stop . . . She came into her powers. Time stopped."

Is that why they called it a trigger? It seemed that a painful event in a magical girl's life caused their powers to activate. I was feeling guilty about dredging up bad memories for Roa when she said, "The Magical Girl of Time . . . She managed to pull herself out of that situation and quickly realized what her power was. There aren't that many magical girls who can control their abilities to the same degree . . ."

I guess she's like those Serengeti animals that can walk as soon as they're born, I thought. It's probably a good thing someone like that became the Magical Girl of Time instead. But . . . If she were untalented but on our side, wouldn't that actually be better than being talented and not on our side?

"Someone was being violent toward her," Roa said. "She froze time and dragged him into the kitchen. It wasn't easy, given their size difference."

"'Kitchen'? You're saying it happened at her house?"

Roa nodded.

"She found the biggest pot she had and filled it with hot water—she probably sped up the process. It started boiling immediately, and then she plunged his head into it and unpaused time."

For a moment, neither I nor Roa said anything.

"And the Magical Girl of Time told you all that?"

"That's what I 'saw.' The moment she realized her powers."

I recalled Roa sitting in that park with her head in her hands. She hadn't experienced it herself, of course, but just having witnessed it must've been traumatic enough. I suddenly felt ashamed of how resentful I'd felt toward her for up and disappearing on me that day.

"I was sorry I had to see it, but once I did, I understood her position better. Why she had to become the Magical Girl of Time, why she's refusing to lend a hand to the union." Then Roa smiled shyly. "Expecting a magical girl to always be good in this world is even less realistic than believing in fairies. Once I understood that . . . Well, it's hard."

It was.

This wasn't a manhwa series; not every magical girl in existence could be good. Doling out love and hope, goodness, and so on; fighting against aliens or evil beings from another world; we were doing none of those things. We were just going through life, getting hurt in body and soul like everyone else. The only thing we had in common with those cartoons was that we couldn't explain our powers in a scientific way; unfortunately, our world was infinitely messier, and here, anyone who fights a magical girl was going to get hurt. Someone was bound to bleed. And that someone might be a person not entirely unlike a magical girl themselves. But we had no choice but to fight. Just as the Magical Girl of Time's origin story shows, the first battle a magical girl must fight is the fight to save herself.

But . . . but . . . what happens if a magical girl has to fight another magical girl? I wondered what Roa meant by her being someone we should be very frightened of not having on our side.

"When we first met, you asked me if one had to be a girl to be a magical girl."

I snapped back to the present and stuttered a yes, whereupon Roa sighed deeply.

"I feel silly calling it a theory, but my theory is this. The world—how do I put this—is trying to find a balance between powers."

"A 'balance'?"

"The reason magical girls exist is because they needed their power the most. In other words, before a magical girl awakens her powers, she's the weakest person in the world."

We were now in front of my apartment. I wanted to ask her in for some tea (not that I had any at home to offer), but given she had just confessed to me, I was a bit too shy to do so.

"Here's what I think," Roa said. "Because these powers are granted to the weakest people, it just looks like girls are the only ones who get to be magical."

Then Roa began walking away. I continued to wave my hand at her back as she became smaller and smaller, disappearing around the bend in the alley. *Just a minute ago, she said she'd protect me, but there she goes without even glancing back.* Pouting, I stepped back into the house, only to wonder if, upon coming to my doorstep, Roa herself had suddenly felt embarrassed about what had just transpired and didn't want to step inside. I mean, for someone who's always taking taxis, she sure spent a lot of time and care to escort me under her umbrella.

Suddenly, I wanted to become the Magical Girl of Weather.

If only it wouldn't rain on Roa's way home, I put my hands together and wished as fervently as possible, but the rain still pattered down on the windowpane. If I was the Magical Girl of Weather, I could be of help to her, and to the union. But that would be getting my hopes up. A little girl hoping it won't rain at her school picnic tomorrow probably has a better chance of becoming the Magical Girl of Weather.

Which reminded me. What magical girl *was* I?

One with a very insignificant ability, probably. My hand fondled the credit card talisman in my pocket, which I didn't even remember bringing with me to the interview.

Roa will find out soon enough, anyway. That someone as cool as her is too good for the likes of me.

The thought made my heart ache.

The Magical Girl
with the Rose

I wonder if, from a distance, something like this could be called "balance." Like, if there's a forest fire on one continent and a huge flood on another. Or if one dot on this planet is extremely hot and dry, another will be as wet and weak as a sheet of paper soaking in the rain. The heat, the cold, the rising ocean levels, the tornadoes, they are all things happening at specific points across this world. Together they form our planet's average temperature and humidity (I guess?).

If we *are* looking at Earth from a distance, it may be hard for us to imagine that there are countless living creatures in each of those tiny dots. Forest fires kill thousands of plants and animals. Hurricanes and tsunamis banish people from their homes, even killing them in extreme cases.

All this stuff has been happening for a long time now. Even if we're not talking about climate disaster here, this planet has water, rotates at a slightly tilted axis, and is circling a gigantic globe made of heat and light—of course things are bound to happen. They also enable life to exist, but what manages to survive keeps struggling to coexist with an enemy too big to fight against, an enemy we call the climate . . .

The climate has always been cruel; we'd be naive to expect mercy from something that doesn't think or feel in the first place. But the reason something so merciless to begin with now has the word "disaster" following it is because it happens to be an enemy we've lived with for thousands of years, one we thought we'd understand by now, but the situation is becoming much more untenable, even further beyond our control. Not only is it getting hotter and colder, but typhoons, which used to be rare in Korea, are passing through all summer long, glaciers are melting so much that land is disappearing before our eyes . . . The most alarming thing about these changes is the speed at which they're happening. It's like a piece of candy in your mouth that melts faster the smaller it gets.

The rain that started when I met Roa did not stop for four days.

Rainwater pooled everywhere, and most certainly in the basement apartment where I lived. Whenever someone opened the front door to the building, the water would cascade down the steps and wash into my foyer. As I mopped it up, I thought, *This rain is going to sink the entire building if it doesn't let up soon.*

As I hung the rag over the back of a chair to dry, I discovered a big black spot in the middle of a wall. I bent over to see whether it was fungus or the remains of a bug I'd killed, but ended up leaning my head against the wall, wiping away tears.

How am I going to go to work tonight?

How amazing it was that people went to work in this rain. Despite the deluge about to swallow us all, the fact that someone kept opening and closing the front door of my complex meant people were commuting to and from work, continuing to live their lives in the apartments upstairs. Working, dropping by the store, all the things they need to do to keep going. I needed to keep going too. If I wanted to be ordinary, I had to put the effort into being ordinary. I just felt annoyed that of all the ordinary things

I had to do, I had to start with the one where I'm going to work in the rain . . .

Keeping the weather in mind, I stepped out a little early. My job gave me a vest to wear over my clothes, so I could wear whatever I wanted, but I was asked to wear long pants and closed-toe shoes. I couldn't walk through the underwater streets in those clothes, so I put them in a bag and stepped out in sandals. The sensation of water coming up to my ankles and flowing against my sandals made my legs feel like boat oars.

The convenience store, of course, was open and running despite the rain.

"Young lady!" the manager said. "I was so worried you wouldn't show up today."

I checked the time; there was just half an hour to go before my shift. After I quickly changed into my pants, switched shoes, and put on my vest, the manager launched into a tirade. She told me that even if I'm being paid by the hour, that didn't mean I should show up right at eight, and that if I had to change clothes, I should've come even earlier, and that I had a lot to learn so I should've come early in the first place . . . I got her point, but the way she delivered it, especially given it was literally my first hour on the job, was too much. I was exhausted already.

The manager told me what needed to be done at what time and what I needed to be careful about. She went on and on until my ears tingled. An hour after I got on shift, the dairy products and ice cream arrived. At midnight, I needed to transfer that day's cash into the safe. No matter what I was doing, as soon as a customer entered the store, I needed to return to the counter. Two a.m. was when the kimbap and sandwiches arrived. I needed to collect them, scan them in, and display them. First in, first out; the ones with closer expiration dates needed to be near the front, so anything new needed to be stacked in the back. Expired products were supposed to be thrown out, but well, the manager was willing to pretend I wouldn't take them home. Kimbap rolls an hour or two past the sell-by date were unsellable but still edible. If I didn't feel like eating them, I could always throw them away. Even though a lot of managers would tell workers to stack food in the back of the fridge so the managers themselves could take stuff home, I was very lucky she wasn't one of those selfish types. While we were on the subject of fridges, the manager told me that she'd restock just about everything during the daytime, but I'd be responsible for handling the drinks. Basically, I had to look over the soda stock at, say, 6:00 a.m. and slip some in if there were empty spaces.

Sure. Yes. Of course. Yes. Yes, I'll do that. Yup!

Lastly, I learned how to use the bathroom. Reenter the building to the left, go up half a floor, and there's a locked bathroom we share with a noraebang; the key is over here, and there's toilet paper inside, but there's no sink so I would have to wash my hands in the staff room . . . I mean, she couldn't stop me from going, but she did recommend I go between 2:00 a.m. and 3:00 a.m., when there were fewer people around.

I'd thought more people would be buying umbrellas, but sales were slow. *Well, I guess it has been raining for a while; no one is going to forget to take their umbrella with them.* I had figured the rainy weekend would keep customers away, but they kept pouring in.

Around 2:00 a.m., the manager began to nod off. She did tell me this was when things would slow down. I'd been thinking it would be a good time to catch some shut-eye—then the manager's phone screen caught my eye. A video about the recent effects of climate change was playing. According to the subtitles, the experts were at a loss to explain this rain coming down, and could only say the climate was changing so quickly we were entering a climate disaster—water levels were rising because the average temperatures were increasing, and the polar ice caps were shrinking. But was that all there was to it . . . ?

Though I wasn't an expert, I had a suspicion this weather may have had something to do with the Magical Girl of Time. Blaming all these recent, sudden changes on her was probably just me being petty, but this weather really seemed like it was her doing.

The video came to an end. The next one, bumped into the playlist by the algorithm, was a little strange. An ordinary-looking woman, so ordinary looking it was hard to tell how old she was, held a rose as she spoke directly into the camera. The video was about two hours long, but it had a remarkable number of hits. Why was it so popular? Judging by what had come before it, did this video have something to do with climate change too?

My curiosity suddenly turned into fear. In an attempt to ask her to turn up the volume, I put my hand on the manager's shoulder, waking her with a start.

"Oh, I must've dozed off." Embarrassed, she wiped the bit of drool from the side of her mouth. "I'll be back in the morning, so we'll go over cleaning up and all that stuff later, okay? Call if there's anything you don't understand."

The manager hastily shrugged off her uniform vest and rushed into the staff room. A few seconds later, she stepped out with her bag in tow, in such a hurry to leave that she didn't even say goodbye. Briefly miffed by her rapid exit, I decided to look up the video I'd just glimpsed. How would I find it? As soon as I picked up my phone and opened a search window, I realized I had nothing to worry about. "Magical Girl of Time" was already trending.

This time, I watched the video with the sound on.

"Hello. My name is Lee Mirae."

Her face looked like she was anywhere from seventeen to twenty-five, but her voice was clearly that of a young girl. The youthfulness of her voice and the adultlike manner of her speech were almost dissonant. I couldn't help but mumble, "How does even her name mean 'future'?" Truly this was someone born to be the Magical Girl of Time.

"I am a survivor of domestic violence. I do not want to define myself in this way, but I need to introduce myself as such for now."

Was that why she was holding that rose? I peered at her closely. In a measured voice, she continued to speak.

"Recently, I came in possession of an inexplicable superpower. To explain it in terms you will be familiar with, I seem to have realized the powers of a magical girl. Specifically, according to what is Korea's largest union and association for magical girls, I am the Magical Girl of Time."

This explained why there were so many hits on the video—a magical girl of her magnitude had revealed her identity online.

"The union has proposed a plan where I save humanity by stopping climate change. Apparently, this is something only the Magical Girl of Time can pull off. As a beginner who has only just discovered her powers, I am very grateful for the confidence they have placed in me but have informed them their proposal is beyond me. And this is what I wish to tell everyone in the Republic of Korea and the world at large."

I remembered what Roa had told me. It would be a fearsome thing if the Magical Girl of Time weren't on our side.

"It is my belief that the world does not need humanity."

Lee Mirae paused for a moment before continuing, "My own suffering led me to this conclusion. But in the grand scheme of things, I think it's the right idea to have. The history of humanity is one of war. Humans harm each other and harm the planet. There is a reason this power was given to someone like me.

"Which is why I wish to use my power to accelerate the end of humanity. You may have your suspicions about my motives. You may even doubt I truly am the Magical Girl of Time. And if you do have such doubts, I urge you to rewatch this video from the very beginning."

What did that mean? Despite the fact that I believed her, I scrolled back to the beginning to watch the video again. Nothing about it had changed. When the video got back to the point where I'd scrolled back, she continued.

"If you understand the power that I hold, you will also understand it is impossible to stop me. I am sending you this message so humanity will realize its past foolishness and prepare itself for the end. Climate change will escalate dramatically from this point on. Thank you to the union for the idea."

Then she put down the rose she was holding. That's when I realized why she had asked us to watch the video from the beginning. I was so focused on her that I hadn't noticed, but by the end of the video, the rosebud had shriveled. The Magical Girl of Time had sped through the rose's entire lifespan.

To prove that she had the power to.

Magical Girl vs. Magical Girl

>You actually believe this? It's fake. She made a time-
lapse video of some flower and edited it in.

>If it's fake, then why are there so many hits?

>The fact that it has so many hits is only proof you're all
idiots.

I gazed at the infinite scroll of arguments in the comments and turned off the video. As one of the few people who knew the Magical Girl of Time had awakened before this video went live (whether this was luck or not, I was unsure), I was way past being skeptical of her claims at this point.

Also, the fact that Lee Mirae filmed this video at all was, if anything, the greatest gesture of generosity she could make as the Magical Girl of Time. Judging by how quickly she mastered her powers, there were crueler and more explicit ways she could've revealed her abilities. For example, she could've rapidly aged a person to death, or sped up time to throw a stone so it'd pass through them like a bullet (maybe that would've gotten the video categorized as a snuff film, and YouTube would have deleted it).

Since she was all about the end of the world, she could've dispensed with the pleasantries and the self-introduction. I mean, surely stopping time and messing with Earth's rotation would've gotten the job done very quickly. She could get rid of all the people on these streets in a second. She was that powerful.

And her thanking the union at the end—that was going to cause a lot of problems for them. My body ached all over, which seemed to come from my worrying over Roa. Should I call her? It was either too late or too early for that. Though, she could be awake and in a crisis meeting. But that was just a guess, and to wake her up when she happened to be asleep would be even worse, especially when she needed her rest now more than ever.

I was feeling too antsy to stand or sit. I paced around the store, wondering if I would be able to survive the coming apocalypse if I was left in a place like this. Then the manager arrived and yelled at me that I should've cleaned up if I wasn't going to take a nap. I should've felt angry about that, but I didn't. We were all going to die, who cared if the store was clean or not? . . . But aside from that, she was supposed to teach me the ins and outs of cleaning and all that junk, and she hadn't. I could've used that against her, but given that the video had kept me up all night, I just didn't have the strength.

After cleaning up the store, which felt like the most useless task in the universe at the moment, I grabbed a kimbap that was a few hours past its sell-by date and left. It was eight in the morning, but still dark because of the rain. While I was at work, I'd worried about how much rainwater had seeped into my apartment, but luckily it turned out it wasn't anything a rag couldn't handle.

I got ready for bed and lay down, but I couldn't fall asleep. *Dammit, I have work tonight too.* I tossed and turned a bit, then looked at my phone: only a half an hour had passed.

And annoyingly enough, "Magical Girl of Time" was still a trending topic on social media. Even though I knew I'd only regret it, I clicked the most popular links underneath the heading. An expert opined there was no way Lee

Mirae's video had been doctored. An organization called the Society Against the Privatization of Magical Girls had published a petition. A world climate watchdog may start an international movement to fight against the Magical Girl of Time . . .

I know she's a magical girl, but she's also just a girl—they can't declare war on her! I sat up and stared into the screen and then lay down again. *All right, now go to sleep, dammit.*

At eleven, a red dot with the word LIVE next to it appeared below the search bar of the portal site I was looking at. The title made it impossible not to click.

NATIONAL TRADE UNION OF MAGICAL GIRLS: PRESS STATEMENT FROM THE CHAIRPERSON

The press conference opened with the chairperson, Yeon Liji, standing by a podium and bowing to the gathered press and public. She was doused with camera flashes. The chairperson straightened her back, went behind the podium, adjusted the microphone, and began to read from her prepared statement in a calm voice.

"To my fellow citizens. The government has requested we answer two questions and allowed us this forum to do so, but beyond answering your questions, we wish to share an additional statement with all of you. I won't be long, so please listen to the end. First, regarding the veracity of the viral video heightening tensions among the public—"

The chairperson said the union had confirmed the existence of the Magical Girl of Time and that Lee Mirae, the girl in the video, was said person. While the whole world knew magical girls walked among us, the chairperson said it was incredibly rare to see a magical girl reveal her identity like this, and that it was not surprising her video would create such a stir. The second question was whether she really did pose as dangerous a threat as she said in the video. (The intent of the question was apparently a request for clarification from the union as to whether the threat should be taken seriously.) For a moment, the chairperson's voice seemed to break before she adjusted her expression and faced the audience again.

"With more than half of the three hundred magical girls active in the country as its members, the National Trade Union of Magical Girls is our nation's representative body for magical girls. Today, I stand here alone, but rest assured my entire organization will put every effort into stopping the Magical Girl of Time."

Answering the question of whether the Magical Girl of Time was a threat with the number of members belonging to the union struck me as strange. While it might mean, having so many members, we have nothing to worry about, it could also imply that this enemy was so powerful we needed all of these girls to work in tandem. In any case, it had become clear that the Magical Girl of Time was someone we were about to find ourselves in confrontation with . . . When I realized this last part, I thought, *Wow*.

"The more important thing now is the question magical girls have already been asking ourselves: How will the world stay safe after this?"

Despite all the flashing cameras that surely must've hurt her eyes, the chairperson continued to speak without blinking.

"Even if the entire union gets together and manages to stave off the Magical Girl of Time, that doesn't mean the climate crisis is over. The countdown to this time bomb has already begun, and she is merely someone who will make it happen faster, not slower. We will need copious amounts of imagination for the problems that lie beyond the defeat of the Magical Girl of Time. It is our role to persuade her to join our cause, but if *your* efforts as well as ours don't bring about a greater change, whether we win or lose is beside the point."

That was the end of her statement. As the reporters began jumping to their feet with questions, covering the camera's line of sight, the live broadcast ended. My heart was pounding with an irregular beat. Asking us to imagine a world beyond the defeat of the Magical Girl of Time seemed to suggest victory was ours, but the conditional "whether we win or lose" made it sound like the opposite. What would happen if we lost? And how was it possible to win against someone who could manipulate time with the crook of an index finger?

That said, the thought of fighting the Magical Girl of Time together wasn't just frightening but repugnant. Despite everything going on, I just couldn't bring myself to think of her as a bad person. Sure, she was a little extreme, but she was living by her convictions—she was only knocking numbers off a clock that was ticking toward a doom of our own making. Again, there were crueler ways she could've gone about it. But to go against Lee Mirae, it felt like the only choice we had was to destroy her. Countless magical girls would have to put their lives on the line for this.

What's going to happen to us . . . I must've fallen asleep thinking this, because my heart began pounding again as soon as I woke up. The union, the Magical Girl of Time, Ah Roa. Names and words flitted through my head; the fact that I'd fallen asleep in spite of everything made me feel so pathetic I snorted with laughter.

"Were you napping?"

I screamed. Roa was crouched on the ground, looking down at me. I wasn't even home, I realized—Roa was surrounded by people. We were in the middle of an eight-lane highway! And there I was, sleeping in the middle of it.

"What . . . where . . . what time . . . *what the hell is going on?*"

As I looked around, I saw the chairperson holding a cordless vacuum cleaner like a guitar, gesturing into the air.

"We've summoned the entire union," Roa explained. "Every magical girl who's received a talisman from the chairperson."

Oh, my talisman . . . I shoved my hand into the pocket of the shorts I wore as pajama bottoms and felt the solid edges of my credit card. Flustered, I just nodded in acknowledgment, watching the other magical girls appear out of thin air. A familiar face popped out right in front of Roa.

"Hey!" said Choi Heejin, seemingly both glad and annoyed to see me. "Don't tell me this is another field trip? Roa, I told you not to bring civilians to these things."

Roa put a hand on her hip and was about to say something, but I butted in.

"It's not a field trip," I said. "I'm here because of my talisman."

"Oh, so unni has a talisman?"

Feeling a little proud of myself, I took out my card and showed it to Choi Heejin.

"What's your power?"

"I'm not sure yet."

"Pfft, that makes you a civilian. Go sit in that corner over there and don't get in our way." Despite having said that, she was the one who left. I waved goodbye at her and turned to Roa.

"Where are we? What's going on?"

"This is our training ground, the Ahgonggan space. Heejin made it for us. Did you see the press conference today?"

"Yes." *And I fell asleep.*

"We have a plan to lure the Magical Girl of Time here to stop her," she whispered to me as if worried someone would overhear.

"Attention!"

It was the chairperson. She slid the vacuum cleaner into her pocket, snapped open a pair of fans, and fanned the ground with them. Her body floated upward. Before I could stop myself, I exclaimed "Wow!" but apparently I was the only one who had never seen her do this.

"Neat, huh?" said Roa. "We have a workshop on flying. You should take it sometime. It's a way of optimizing our abilities. You have to be very creative about how you take flight."

"Can you fly too?"

"Well, it's more like I try to crash with as little chance of dying as possible . . . but I guess that is a form of flying."

The chairperson fanned herself up until she was high enough for all the magical girls to see her.

"Our mission is to bring the Magical Girl of Time here alive. Ms. Yu Dasom! Bring the magical girls before me as I call them."

The strategy was as follows: Roa would use her clair-voyance to predict where the Magical Girl of Time would be. The Magical Girl of Heart, Bae Jinhee (she seemed to be telepathic), would inform the union; Choi Heejin would create a portal right behind her; and Cha Minhwa, the Magical Girl of Scent, would knock her out with an anesthetic.

Since Roa was the first one mentioned, she was midway into explaining who Yu Dasom was when she started float-ing upward and away.

Choi Heejin, Cha Minhwa, and Yu Dasom were on the summoning team; once the Magical Girl of Time was in the Ahgonggan, the chairperson would attempt to re-negotiate. In the event of the worst-case scenario, they would then summon magical girls from around the world to the cause.

Choi Heejin raised her hand and screeched, "Then why bother bringing her here alive? Why can't we just kill her?"

"Because we still need her power. We can't just give up on the Magical Girl of Time."

I doubt Lee Mirae's going to go down without a fight. But I couldn't agree with the violent alternative of killing her either. What was Choi Heejin's problem? Was she salty because there was a magical girl more powerful than her? When she herself already had so much power?

The chairperson raised her voice once again.

"Don't forget—the Magical Girl of Time may be formidable, but she doesn't know what we are capable of. Now is the time to strike. And we only have this one chance."

The Worst Magical Girl in the World

Roa took out her Ahroamirror and showed the chairperson and the Magical Girl of Heart what was inside. They seemed to have figured out where the Magical Girl of Time was. The Magical Girl of Heart brought her hands together like in prayer, and the rest of the magical girls, including the ones floating above us, brought their hands to their ears to listen to what she had to say. Then they all nodded in unison—but I hadn't heard a thing. *I mean, I just have a talisman. It's not like I'm a member of the union. No one's calling me a magical girl.* I nodded to myself, a gesture toward something different from what everyone else was nodding to. Like someone pretending not to notice the king was naked, I was about to rub my ears but then thought better of it. Being caught in a lie would be more embarrassing.

The chairperson brought out two gas masks and gave them to Choi Heejin and Yu Dasom. Heejin put hers on while gesturing and created a door, stamping her feet in the air impatiently while waiting for Dasom to put hers on properly. Once Dasom was all set, she gave a thumbs-up and Heejin opened the door. Cha Minhwa, Heejin, and Dasom entered one by one.

Bae Jinhee put her hand on the Ahroamirror, and the three magical girls' actions were projected above us in the Ahgonggan for all to see. The room they were in looked like that of a typical teenage girl from a TV drama. There was a desk with a shelf in the shape of a lowercase h, one of those wheeled Duoback chairs, a big bed strewn with cushions and stuffed animals . . . I almost found myself saying out loud, *Her life seems ordinary enough from the outside. I guess abuse happens even in houses that look like this.* The moment I thought that, the chair suddenly popped out from the desk and swiveled around.

There sat the Magical Girl of Time, Lee Mirae.

The hologram looked so real that every magical girl gasped in surprise. *Whew, they're using the anesthetic*—even my most immediate thought seemed to be shared among us, judging from the audible sighs of relief that followed.

When hit with Cha Minhwa's magic fragrance, Lee Mirae looked as though she was looking at us but also as if she was staring into space. Dasom gestured, and the chairperson rolled toward the other magical girls inside the room. Heejin reopened the door and Minhwa came back first. Dasom gestured, making Mirae float through the opening. Even a civilian like me could sense the change of mood in the room. I could feel the magical girls' hackles rising. Dasom and Heejin followed after Mirae, and the door in the air disappeared. Roa and Jinhee stopped their holographic projection.

"Ms. Yu Dasom, leave only Ms. Lee Mirae before me. Ms. Cha Minhwa, let Ms. Lee Mirae speak."

Under her command, Minhwa placed a hand on Mirae's throat and the other magical girls who were part of the mission, excluding the chairperson and Mirae, floated back down to us. Roa ran toward me and grabbed my hand. Together, we gazed up at the scene above us.

The chairperson sighed.

"All right, then," she said. "Let's talk."

"You've gathered a mob and kidnapped me here and want to talk? You're joking."

Wow, I thought, *she really has no fear or respect. I mean, the chairperson is an elder, after all . . .* On the one hand, I knew what Mirae was saying wasn't right, but on the other hand, all things considered, I got a strong sense she had been more than respectful about her plan to end humanity. If you really thought about it.

"We're engaging in an intervention." There was a slight tremor in the chairperson's voice. "I've already told you that the Magical Girl of Time would be so powerful that we wouldn't be able to control her through normal means. All we can do is hope for the goodwill of the one blessed with such power."

Just then, Roa tugged my hand and whispered, "By the way, if this doesn't work out—"

I was so engrossed with what was going on above us that I only glanced at her and said, "Oh, sure—" before looking back, only to have Roa squeeze my hand and speak to me in an even more urgent whisper.

"I need you to become the most selfish person in the world. Only think of your own survival. All right?"

What is she talking about? I thought, *What's the point of telling the most insignificant person here that?* Besides, we were surrounded by powerful magical girls and the most

128

powerful magical girl was half-incapacitated anyway. How bad could things possibly get?

"Okay, okay—" I shook her hand, but Roa did not respond. She was trembling like the chairperson—only then did I remember that Roa could see the future.

"Wait, did you—"

Just as I was about to ask her if she had a bad premonition, the magical girls began to scream. I looked up again.

Mirae was holding up her arm.

"Of course, I remember everything you said to me."

She sounded as calm and mature as she did in her apocalyptic viral video.

"I think you're the one who doesn't remember. Because this is what I recall—magical girls with invisible powers can do a lot with just their thoughts."

Come to think of it, while I had been listening to Roa, I hadn't heard a peep out of the chairperson. Had she . . . ? Was she unable to talk because Mirae froze the chairperson in time . . . ?

As if to answer my question, the chairperson began to fall. Dasom must've used her power because the chairperson stopped just before she crashed into the ground, but the sight of it was enough to make my heart plunge. The magical girls raised their arms and adopted a combat pose.

"To tell me I have the power to save the world, and then provoke me," Mirae said. "You overestimated me at first, and now you underestimate me. I've been waiting for this moment when all the magical girls would be in one place. Thanks for making this so easy."

"Shut up, you crazy bitch!"

It was Heejin. A door had appeared right behind Mirae. Heejin jumped out of it, shoved Mirae inside, closed the door, and landed.

"Miss Big Shot's acting real cocky for someone who can't even control crowds."

She was making a big show of dusting off her hands, when Mirae reappeared right in front of her.

"It's too bad they don't pick magical girls for their intelligence."

"Wh-what—"

"I'm the Magical Girl of Time," she said with a smile. "Hitting rewind is a piece of cake. To think you can't even get that straight."

Heejin didn't answer Mirae. She couldn't—she was frozen in time. Mirae was still smiling.

"That power to control crowds? Who needs that? I can still take on you all at once. How shall I put this in terms you understand . . . I command time to stop for all the magical girls in this space."

With a dramatic flair, she flicked her finger in the air. Suddenly, the hand desperately holding on to mine felt different. A bit harder, colder . . . Not dead but . . . frozen.

"I think I've been very nice about things, you know. I can make your hearts stop at the same time, but I'm not doing that. How much nicer do you want me to be? Aren't you being a little greedy, asking for more?"

Mirae clasped her hands behind her back and walked among the petrified crowd.

"Paralysis. That was the first ability I unlocked when I realized my powers. Paralysis means pausing time in a physical sense. If I want to undo paralysis, I can make time flow quicker."

Mirae came to a stop before a short magical girl. Ahn Subin. The giant of the Heathrow Airport incident. Apparently preparing to attack, her right arm was enlarged but frozen. Mirae grinned.

"That's not the only thing I've learned. If I stop time and enact paralysis, a person's mind and senses will also stop. Which is why the first person I killed probably felt no pain."

Mirae walked around, looking at each magical girl like she was touring a hall of mannequins.

"It was such a shame. I really wanted him to feel it."

She passed me. The way she was practically swinging her shoulders at this point looked like she was flaunting her mobility. *Of course she would. She thinks she's the only person who can move right now.*

I was worried a bead of sweat rolling down my face would give me away.

Because she was wrong. She wasn't the only one who could move.

I was not a magical girl and hence did not fall under her spell that applied to "all of the magical girls in this space."

I felt like I was in a game of Red Light, Green Light and "it" was looking back for a little too long. In that moment, my entire being was about to twitch and spasm.

"So I've gotten some practice. What do you think? Can everyone hear me okay? I stopped your bodies but not your minds."

Mirae walked right by me; she didn't seem to have noticed anything was off. I kept still, flicking my eyes toward Roa. The magical girl that she was, she was frozen stiff.

"If any of you have mind-based powers, do your worst. I don't like to win too easily."

Despite my fervent hopes, no one rose to the challenge. I guess it was understandable, but then again, were there really so few magical girls with invisible powers?

I kept looking at Roa, her other hand that was not gripping mine. She was holding the mirror. My face was reflected inside it. Just like on that day when I had tried to kill myself.

If this doesn't work out, I need you to become the most selfish person in the world.

Had Roa seen the future unfolding right before us? Is that why she said what she said?

And why me?

"It is pretty convenient I can destroy everyone at once, but I have no idea what to do with you all. It's not like I can put it to a vote or anything. There are just so many options. But I detest blood, so nothing bloody."

Mirae kept droning on. I just . . . couldn't find a path to "survival," as Roa had mentioned. There was no real way for me to escape, and even if I did manage to find a hiding place, I couldn't hide from a magical girl who had infinite stores of time on her hands. If I couldn't defeat the Magical Girl of Time on my own, then there was no way I could make it out of here alive. Whereas if I *did* defeat her, then I could help Roa, the chairperson, Heejin, Subin, Dasom, Minhwa . . . I could save everyone. Which meant the most selfish choice I could make was also the least self-ish one.

But how to pull it off?

I frowned as the bead of sweat began making its way down my forehead. I finally wanted to defeat someone in battle, and it just so happened that someone was unde-featable.

Then, I felt a warmth spreading in my pocket. My eyes looked down. There were strands of light coming out of my shorts. I suddenly understood what it meant. Some-thing similar had happened recently. I was awakening my power. Now, of all times, when I must not be found out by my undefeatable enemy.

What was going to happen to me?

How to Defeat a Magical Girl

I heard Mirae's footsteps pause. The light shining out of my credit card was so intense it was wrapping around my body (and Roa's intertwined hand), causing the magical girls around me to throw shadows, which caught Mirae's attention.

Rapid footsteps approached.

I was about to cry. Why was I awakening my powers now, when I hadn't been able to back when I'd tried so hard? Was it because I wanted to defeat the Magical Girl of Time that badly? Because I'd dared try on shoes that were too big for my feet? It just wasn't fair. The pressure from the anger and fear were forcing tears to my eyes.

"You . . ."

Mirae looked me up and down, fascinated. As if to make a point, my body began floating in the air (still desperately gripping Roa's hand), and the light was changing the shape of my clothes. I was transforming when I hadn't even chanted a spell . . . Mirae's amused staring couldn't be more humiliating. It angered me. A magical girl's first transformation should not make her want to die.

"So this is a magical girl transformation sequence," Mirae said. "How entertaining."

I had descended, and when I looked down at myself, I was wearing a beautifully tailored black suit, the kind I had never worn before or even dared to want, or maybe I did in my heart of hearts—it was a very nice version of a suit a working person would wear. Even with the fate of humanity in my hands, I was glad that I didn't have to wear a super frilly aurora borealis princess dress like Roa's.

"Why didn't my spell work on you?"

"Well," I said reluctantly, although there was no need to make a secret of it, really, "I wasn't a magical girl until a moment ago."

"Really? How bizarre."

Though her oddly adult manner of speaking struck me as more bizarre than what had just happened, I tried my best not to scoff—but it was Mirae who looked like she was barely holding in her laughter.

"So you don't happen to know what your ability is?"

". . . No."

She burst into laughter, her hands on her belly. My fear was shoved aside by annoyance. She was being such a . . . what's the word I'm looking for?

She's being such a dick.

She laughed a bit more and finally, still smiling, said, "My mistake. I should've said everyone in this space, not just magical girls. But how was I to know there would be a civilian in here? Maybe calling it a 'mistake' is too much."

Annoyed and hurt, I grabbed my credit card and brandished it in her face.

"What's that?"

"My . . . weapon."

She burst into laughter again. So hard this time that she collapsed on the ground and had to hold on to a nearby petrified magical girl for support. She found my talisman to be that hilarious.

"Are you . . . Are you insane?" she asked.

Now I was about to burst into tears for an entirely different reason.

"What do you plan to do with that thing—you're going to *charge* me to death? Chop me up into twelve low-interest installments? You're not some kind of comedian, are you?"

I tried to hold back my tears at her snark.

Look, I don't know what I'm supposed to do with this thing, I thought. *But the thing is, I could've been you. I could've become the Magical Girl of Time. If that had happened, I wouldn't have mocked you the way you're mocking me now. And you wouldn't have been able to save yourself. Perhaps it's because I'm so stupid, so useless that you could even become you. So, if you'll allow me to make a bit of a leap here, you're this powerful because of me. And you don't even know that.*

But here you are, treating me like dirt.

"Anyway," she went on, "who knows what you're capable of. How about we nip this in the bud?"

She flicked a finger, and my entire body froze. I was still aware, but I couldn't speak or shift my gaze. I was frozen in my stupid pose of trying to shove my credit card up her nose.

"Thank you for that last bit of comedy."

Mirae skipped and swam up into the air. She was flying. That was the way the Magical Girl of Time flew—a little skip, freeze time, skip up from there, freeze time before falling . . . If I could sigh in that moment, I would've. She was using skills no one had taught her. *What a genius. Quite dickish, but she's a clever one. A born magical girl. Not only is she the most powerful of us all, but she's even a genius.*

Whereas I . . . may have had the stupidest power awakening in the history of magical girls. I can't do anything right; I don't even know what I'm capable of! Not just as a magical girl but as a person in general.

"That last magical girl I defeated—I forget what her ability was—gave me a great idea. I shall end all of you now."

Mirae was up high somewhere, shouting down at us. Was this really the end? *I'm so sorry, Roa. I'm so sorry, Madam Chairperson, all the magical girls . . . I was the last one of us standing, but I was hopeless . . .*

I wanted to close my eyes, but I couldn't. I wanted to cry, but of course, being frozen got in the way of that. *I'm sorry*—I wanted to say it out loud, but . . . *Hope.* I don't know why that vague, ridiculous word suddenly popped into my mind.

What had been the thoughts inside my head right before I realized what my power was?

I had been thinking I couldn't defeat the Magical Girl of Time. I couldn't win, but I wanted to win. I wanted to win . . . *Want.* A desperate hope would present a magic girl with a path toward awakening her powers. In an act of balance, the universe conferred power on those who had the least, and that was why magical girls existed.

If that is the case, I need to use my mystery power to defeat Mirae.

Mirae, for whatever reason, was holding one arm aloft. I suddenly had a bad feeling about what would happen when she lowered it.

Think of something, think! What can I do? How can I defeat the Magical Girl of Time? Nothing in the world could escape the force of time; she could reverse even the most fatal injury I'd inflict on her! How could I ever hope to defeat someone with a power like hers?

I felt like she was lowering her arm in slow motion.

Time, I need time, time to think, but I'm not the Magical Girl of Time, she is, dammit. At the very least, I wish she wasn't the Magical Girl of Time. What am I even—

Wait a minute.

My talisman began to shine, meaning I was somewhere close to the truth.

So that she couldn't use the powers of time . . . No, something clearer . . .

I wish Mirae was no longer the Magical Girl of Time.

Would that work? There's no time—I should try an exclamation point!

I wish Mirae was no longer the Magical Girl of Time!

The moment I made my wish, light exploded from my talisman, and I could see Mirae's arm rising again through the intensity.

"N—!"

No, I was trying to scream, but my voice felt funny, so I touched my throat. And then realized I *could* touch my throat, which meant my arm could move, which meant her power of stopping time was no longer working. The light was so strong, I waved my arms in front of me. Someone grabbed my hand and intertwined our fingers.

"Looking for me?"

"Roa!"

I barely had time to rejoice in her recovery as the Ahgonggan began to shake and break apart. Through the cracks of the walls and ceiling, which had looked like they were made of light, I could see a black blacker than any black I had seen—pure nothingness.

I was frightened. "Something's wrong—"

"Nothing is wrong," said Roa.

The very ground we were standing on was beginning to melt away, but Roa's voice remained calm.

"You did wonderfully."

I fell and fell and fell, then closed my eyes.

The earthquake stopped.

I'm alive? I'm alive . . . I didn't fall anywhere.

I just felt slightly disoriented, like I'd dreamed of falling and had woken up with a start. It was raining. I released the grip I had on my own head and opened my eyes. It was night, I was on the rooftop of a building, and there were about a hundred other women standing around me looking as dazed as I was.

"What happened?" I asked.

"The Ahgonggan collapsed and we were all sent to the roof," Roa said.

"The Ahgonggan . . . Did I do something wrong?"

"No, you did something so, so right. Um, the Ahgonggan collapsing is a little complicated to explain . . ."

The chairperson was wandering among the girls and helping them up. A bunch of magical girls were standing around and looking at something. As the chairperson approached, they made way for her, and Roa and I were able to see what it was.

It was Mirae, lying there unconscious.

I beat her . . . A chill ran down my spine. It didn't feel as good as I thought it would. All I felt was relief that we hadn't required a bigger sacrifice. But what had I done to warrant such a victory?

Wait, if I really did just save the world, then I have bigger problems right now!

"What time is it?" I asked Roa.

"A little after ten, why?"

All my strength left my body. I could only scoff. "My shift started hours ago."

Roa patted my back. "It's a tale as old as time. The hero who saves the world is always the one who loses their job in the end."

The rain began to let up.

A Magical Girl Retires

Ａnd from that day forward, the Magical Girl of Time was powerless," said the chairperson. She cleared her throat and asked, "May I ask how you did it?"

I fiddled with my teacup in its saucer. "I just wished for it," I replied in a small voice. "I just wished she wasn't the Magical Girl of Time anymore."

"You wished for it?"

Everyone sitting there gave a sigh or a gasp or a scoff. The sudden respiration being expelled into the air created a tremor across the surface of my tea.

"Then is she the Magical Girl of Wishes?"

"That sounds a little too vague."

This meeting was to determine whether the Magical Girl of Time really was vanquished and to figure out what to call me. It was like a job interview, I guess. I looked around at the executive-level magical girls and Roa. Roa mouthed, *Don't be nervous.*

I tentatively raised my hand and spoke up.

"Uh, if it's helpful . . . I can demonstrate my power for you."

"Here?"

I could feel the tension in the air. Sure, they only knew me as a magical girl who had taken away another person's power, and that was bound to make them nervous. But my ability really wasn't anything like that.

To not give them any more time to think about it, I brought out my talisman and said, "I want the cheapest five-hundred-milliliter bottle of water you can find."

A water bottle appeared before me, and I tapped my phone to open my internet banking app, then placed it on the table so everyone could see.

"If I ask for a bottle of water, my wish will come true in the most reasonable and cheapest way possible. I always pay the price. The money is deducted from my bank account, in my hands is a water bottle, but I haven't moved a muscle. The cashier at the store probably has my credit card transaction on file. And if I get a refund, they'll have that on file as well."

The chairperson steepled her fingers in front of her and, with a voice coming deep from her diaphragm, murmured, "A magical girl who pays the price . . ."

"If I ask for something ridiculously expensive, like a ring from Tiffany's or a watch from Cartier, I might find myself missing a kidney or a cornea. I don't have the money to buy those kinds of things."

"Can't you ask for your kidney and cornea back?"

"If I do, the ring and watch would be taken away. Or another organ."

"So, you can have anything you please, but the risk is that you don't know what price you'll pay?"

I glanced at Roa and then nodded.

". . . Yes."

"You know," said Roa, "many magical girls seem to have lost their powers or found them diminished that day—maybe all of them. For example, the Ahroamirror is just an ordinary mirror now."

Maybe that's why the Ahgonggan collapsed as well. Choi Heejin owned the space, and now she's powerless.

"Maybe as a price for the Magical Girl of Time giving up her powers, most magical girls had to give up some of their power as well. To maintain the balance of magical power in the world. We'll have to wait and see if they'll recover one day."

"Perhaps."

The older magical girls, who usually had little occasion to put their powers to use, seemed not to have noticed that their powers had diminished until then.

"But what about *her* powers?" said one of them, meekly pointing at me.

"My powers aren't strictly *my* powers. I can only do what I do if I can afford to do it."

I put my credit card in my pocket.

"Which is why I plan on never using my powers ever again."

The other magical girls looked at me in shocked silence.

"I think . . . if there's a danger of putting myself and others in harm's way . . . then I shouldn't use my powers. We were lucky this time, but there's no guarantee that'll always be the case. There aren't that many magical girls left to sacrifice. So . . . I know it hasn't been long since I've come into my powers, but . . . I think the best thing for me to do is to retire."

No one could convince me otherwise. Of course, this was the first time a magical girl had ever retired. Not to mention the magical girl in question had vanquished the most powerful magical girl in history. There was no way they could force me to do anything against my will.

As we left the union office, Roa asked, "Are you sure you won't regret it?"

Well. If the Clairvoyant Magical Girl is asking me that, it sounds like someday I will.

Even though I knew that Roa could no longer predict the future.

"I think I'll be too busy to."

It was true. I was fired from my convenience store job, but the internet café called back. They had said they wanted me to work with them for as long as I could, and they weren't wrong—the hours were pretty long and exhausting. But there I was, looking for extra gigs in supermarkets and retail event support. I wanted to save up as much money as quickly as possible.

To be honest, I was kind of lying when I said I would never use my powers again. It wouldn't hurt anyone to wish for things like wanting the ramyun to boil more quickly, and the café owner and guests thought I was amazing for bringing them their food faster than anyone else. Maybe the gas bill might be slightly more expensive because of it, but that was being paid by the owner, which allowed me to use my abilities without worrying too much. Sometimes I'd be so tired I'd wish I were less so, or I'd wish I felt like I just woke up from a long, deep sleep, and on certain mornings I'd find a clump of my hair falling out or my whole body swelled up. But that wasn't too terrible a price.

These little fixes helped me save time here and there, which made me think I might have become the Magical Girl of Time after all.

So what happened to the real Magical Girl of Time, Lee Mirae? Roa told me she was under the protection of the union.

"She can't ever go back to her previous life. But at the end of the day, she's just your average girl. We're trying to help her live as normally as possible."

I could not bring myself to ask whether that was what Mirae wanted for herself.

But aside from that, wasn't the union in a bit of a weird situation itself, given not everyone had their powers anymore? Roa had an answer for that too.

"There's a sudden surge of people who want to test into the union."

That was unexpected.

"There's an increase in people with magic," explained Roa, "not enough to become magical girls, but pretty significant nonetheless. It might be an aftereffect of that battle. Instead of taking away the power of just one magical girl, the universe reclaimed the magic of several and distributed their power among a wider range of people. But that's just my theory."

I knew Roa was always right, so I simply nodded.

"It got me thinking that it's going to take the little bits of magic that a group of good individuals happen to have to fight against climate change. We might pivot the organization toward becoming an environmentalist group. Mirae created enemies not just for herself but for magical girls in general. Like crime organizations. This is why magical girls everywhere need protection, even if that protection comes from magical girls who don't have much power. But we've got to keep that part secret for as long as we can."

Having answered my questions, Roa clasped my hand again and asked, "So what are your retirement plans?"

It was a question that made me think I had suddenly aged overnight; I grinned. There was no plan. *Make lots of money. A lot of money.* Of course, no one was going to get rich working at an internet café, but it wasn't like I was going to work as a part-timer until the day I died. I was going to pay off my credit card debt and go back to school. There was a dream I had long before I had wanted to become a magical girl, a dream I'd had with far more yearning than awakening my magical girl powers—that's what I was going back to school for.

If I could become a magical girl at twenty-nine, then surely it was never too late to become a watchmaker. But how do I even begin to explain it?

I entwined my fingers in Roa's as I tried to make out the words.

"You know, I've actually had this one dream since I was a child, and it's all I've ever dreamed about . . ."

Much later, I realized it had been ages since I had told my dream to anyone who wasn't my grandfather.

The End

A Note from the Translator

"'Roa'?" I repeated back to my brother years ago when he told me the ultrarare name he was going to give my new niece. "How would you even write that in Hanja?"

Suffice it to say, I took on translating *A Magical Girl Retires* because it had a main character named Roa. I love Park Seolyeon's work, and I would've been on board with anything she had produced with her pen. But when I discovered the spectacularly princessy, kind, empathetic, and intelligent Ah Roa in these pages, I knew that of all the working Korean literary translators in the world, I had to be the one to translate this book. It was as if this fictional Roa had looked into her trusty Ahroamirror and seen my face.

Like many narratives with a seemingly light and fantastical touch, there is a fair bit of darkness hiding in plain sight in *A Magical Girl Retires*, such as the fact that the book begins with a suicide attempt and throughout hints at the dark realities young women face while living in Korea. It is a trying or even traumatic event that awakens a magical girl's powers for the first time, which means every magical girl in this book—and there are quite a few of them—had something terrible happen in their lives at one point or another.

When you're living in Korea, as I am, you are constantly fed media reports of violence against women, a phenomenon made even more disconcerting by the lack of consequences for the perpetrators, even in the face of stark and overwhelming evidence. In *A Magical Girl Retires*, the universe has a way of balancing the scales of power and justice: the power of one magical girl may flow to another to redress the balance, or a girl in peril is given the exact superpower she needs to lift herself out of it to safety. The most iconic magic girl of all, Sailor Moon, specifically refers to herself as a champion of *justice*. The magic that magical girls want is not to grow into giants or concoct powerful fragrances or manipulate time or be clairvoyant—it's the power of justice. Magical girls exist because justice does not.

In a way, of all the powers that appear in this book, our main character's odd-seeming power of (spoiler alert) "paying the price" is the most fantastical of them all. In our world, so many people never face consequences for their actions. Justice is not a given—it is earned. The climate crisis, which throws its shadow across the events that unfold in this book, was created by generations of people who won't have to deal with the worst yet to come. Our descendants will have to pay the climate bill *we* racked up; my niece Roa will grow up in a world with more destructive weather and decreased resources—like breathable air and drinkable water—because of actions that happened long before she was even born.

But for justice to exist, we have to imagine it first. It has to find form, even if that form is as fragile and amorphous as that of a story. A story that is like the Ahroamirror, something that can show us who the hero is. Or that the person who has the power to tell the story, to shape it, and to pass it on was *you* all along.

We do not have the power to turn back time, to change the past. But we have the power to change the future. We have the power, in big ways and small, to enact justice, which in turn means every single one of us is capable of becoming a magical girl. And I hope that empowerment is what the reader, especially my niece, takes away from this book.

—*Anton Hur*
October 2023

A Note from the Illustrator

I'm delighted to have drawn the cover of the English edition of Park Seolyeon's *A Magical Girl Retires*. She excels in portraying the real-life issues we face with a keen eye, and *A Magical Girl Retires* is no exception.

For the cover of this book, I aimed to depict an image of the "magical girl" that many of us have loved since childhood. Ribbons, magical tools, lace decorations . . . but among them, I tried to capture the distinctive, determined, and clear gaze that magical girls possess.

Since I too grew up reading magical girl comics, recalling that time in my life made the cover design process even more joyful. From the drafting stage to putting the final touches on the art, my heart was filled with excitement.

I hope that the comic panels that appear in each chapter of the book will add another layer of enjoyment for readers. While *A Magical Girl Retires*'s story is grounded in some of life's painful realities, it never loses its humor. Translating these scenes from the book into comics was a particularly delightful task.

We've all had a moment in life where we wished we could be magic. I hope this cover might activate your nostalgia and reconnect you to those moments. In fact, we might already be just as supernatural as the magical girl on this cover. Living through today without magic proves it!

—*Kim Sanho*
October 2023

About the Author

Park Seolyeon was born in Cheorwon, South Korea. She made her debut by winning the journal *Silcheon Munhak*'s new author prize and received the 2018 Hankyoreh Literary Award for her novel *The Woman Who Climbed on the Roof*. Her works include the novels *Martha's Job* and *The Shirley Club*, as well as the short story collections *Your Mom's the Better Player* and *Me, Me, Madeline*. She is the recipient of a 2023 Yi Sang Literary Award and the 2021 Munhakdongne Young Writers Award. She is based in Seoul, and *A Magical Girl Retires* is her English debut.

Here ends Park Seolyeon's
A Magical Girl Retires.

The first edition of this book was printed
and bound at LSC Communications in
Harrisonburg, Virginia, in April 2024.

A NOTE ON THE TYPE

The text of this novel was set in Dante, a typeface
designed by Giovanni Mardersteig after the end of
World War II, when his private press, Officina Bodoni,
resumed operations. Influenced by the Monotype
Bembo and Centaur typefaces, Mardersteig wanted
to design a font that balanced italic and roman
harmoniously. Originally hand cut by Charles Malin, it
was adapted for mechanical composition by Monotype
in 1957. Dante remains a popular typeface today, and
it appears especially elegant on the printed page.

HARPERVIA

An imprint dedicated to publishing international voices,
offering readers a chance to encounter other lives and other
points of view via the language of the imagination.